Birthing Pains

By

Cassandra Stout

1

"How do they keep finding us," Turner demanded breathlessly of Theo. Leaning up against a large rock, he worked to quickly reload his weapon. He'd never felt so weary in all his life, "We've been on the run for five long months; everyone is exhausted."

"Ned and I discovered the answer to that three nights ago," Theo began sounding winded.

"Get down," Turner ordered as he aimed the dragon at a jeep that was quickly approaching their location.

Two men were in the vehicle. The driver and another one standing on the passenger side. He was spraying the area with bullets from his machine gun.

He was about to pull the trigger when he heard Kenny's weapon explode. The man wielding the machine gun went down. Turner quickly took out the driver, eliminating the threat, for now.

Breathing a silent sigh of relief, he faced Theo. “How do we stop this; we need time to rest?” Turner inquired knowing full well; if he was this tired, the others had to be about to drop as well.

Standing, Theo motioned for the others to gather around. And then he spoke to them in a loud whisper, “There’s a cabin just across the road. We need to get there quickly so we can put an end to this onslaught.”

“I’ll go first,” Turner informed the team, feeling hopeful that this ordeal might be over soon. “When I’m sure it’s clear; I'll signal you to come across one at a time. Lex, I want you to bring up the rear.”

“Will do,” Lex assured, his eyes carefully scanning the area.

Giving his wife a quick hug, he smiled reassuringly at her, yet he couldn’t help wondering if they would survive this night. Swallowing hard, he crept out of the trees to the edge of the small two-lane highway. This was the darkest night he could remember. There was no moon, and they were miles away from any city illuminations.

He wondered how Theo could be so sure they were near this cabin he mentioned. There were no lights of any kind. They’d run blindly through the woods for hours trying their best not to get themselves killed. Nevertheless, he'd been in many situations with Theo over the years where the man just seemed to know things. He'd come to rely on his instinctive abilities.

Slipping silently across the road, he stopped to listen. The only sound he heard was a lone owl. It seemed too quiet, which gave him pause. Yet he knew they needed to hurry so he ignored his misgivings. He signaled for the others to join him. One by one they scurried toward him. Lex came over last, carefully perusing the area as he went.

"How far is it to the cabin," Kenny whispered sounding uncharacteristically exhausted.

"It should be about twenty yards east of here," Theo informed after quickly glancing at his smart phone.

The light from the phone could serve as a beacon to those who were hunting them. For that very reason, they used it only when absolutely necessary.

"Okay," Turner sighed as he wiped the sweat from his forehead with the sleeve of his Jean jacket. "Let's be on our guard, keeping all directions covered, and yet moving as swiftly as possible," he whispered.

Using hand signals, he instructed Kenny to scan to the right. He then motioned for Lily to cover the left, and Lex to guard the rear while he patrolled the area in front. Taking the lead, they moved out in a diamond formation, keeping Theo, Ned and Cindy protected in the center.

"Stop where you are," came a commanding deep male voice with a thick Spanish accent from out of the darkness.

Turner stopped immediately, as did the others. The next sound they heard was the chambering of several weapons. By the sound of it they were surrounded. Squeezing his eyes closed briefly, Turner wondered if their subsequent breath would be in heaven. He'd thought it was deathly quiet. Why hadn't he trusted his instincts? He required of himself.

"Hand over your weapons," the voice demanded.

"Do what they say," Theo encouraged.

Reluctantly each member of the team handed their guns to the person nearest them.

"Now get going, straight ahead with your hands in the air where we can see them. Don't make any stupid moves."

These men were dressed fully in black with ski masks covering most of their faces. Turner's mind was racing, playing out several possible scenarios of how they might escape. He hated having let everyone down, especially his wife. He had to do something to make this right.

Charging at the man leading them through the woods, Turner knocked him to the ground and wrestled his rifle away from him. However, before he could get to his feet, the man punched him first in the jaw, and then in the stomach. He was powerful and Turner, literally saw stars.

"Stop it," Kenny cried and ran to cover him with her own body.

Two of the men aimed their rifles at Kenny, "Return the weapon to us now!"

Without hesitation, he reached the gun to the man he'd tackled. "To make sure you don't make any more mistakes; the young lady will walk with me. Get him up," he said then to the men who'd threatened his wife.

They hoisted him up and held his arms as they walked on either side of him. His biggest problem was that he, like the others, was dog-tired. They'd done nothing but fight and run for months. If Theo hadn't secured a large cache of ammo before leaving Panama City, they'd be dead already.

They walked along in silence until reaching the cabin. To Turner's surprise, they unlocked the door and ushered them inside. Flipping on the lights, the man holding Kenny took her to a large metal box and placed her in it and latched the door. There was a small window covered with wire mesh where Kenny could peer out.

At this point the men removed their masks.

"Miguel," Theo greeted the man sounding relieved, "Thank you, my friend," he said and hugged him.

"What's going on here," Turner demanded suspiciously of his mentor. "He threatens your niece and you embrace him," Turner bit out angrily.

"I will explain it all to you, but I couldn't until Kenny was safely inside the Faraday cage. Please just listen," Theo entreated, "I need to make this quick.

"As you know, they've been on us relentlessly since Kenny was discharged from the hospital, and we left Panama City. Ned and I decided that they must have tagged one of us somehow. We started scanning everything we had with us, from bullets to underwear. We found nothing."

"So," Ned broke in, "We covertly started scanning the members of the team while you were sleeping. Three nights ago, we hit pay dirt. Remember when we rescued Kenny from the Nephilim?"

"Yeah," Turner answered warily as he rubbed his sore jaw.

"She had several smaller injuries, scrapes and cuts. We assumed they were either from being slung into the pylons after the explosion, or during the battle with the super soldiers at the abandoned military instillation." Ned continued.

"And then, there was the fact that she lost the baby," Theo said sadly. "We were mourning the loss rather than thinking of what they might have done while they held her captive."

"What did they do," Turner inquired, dread sounding in his voice.

"On the pad of the little finger on her left hand, they implanted a sophisticated RFID device. It's made from a flexible silicone material that looks and feels like human skin. We found it supports a high data speed, so we believe they heard everything we said. That's how they could track our movements so quickly. It's far beyond anything made by man.

"And" Theo said and frowned, "it appears to contain a lethal dose substance. That's why we didn't mention to anyone what our plan was, or what we'd learned. If I could have safely warned you not to attack Miguel, I would have. However, we had to keep up the ruse until we could disrupt the transmission. A microwave oven is a type of Faraday cage. It permits the owner to cook the food within, without allowing the microwaves to escape and injure the user. So, I reasoned that the cage could stop any transmission from passing through. Even so; this technology is far beyond our knowledge. We need to remove it as soon as possible."

"Well, do it," Turner said nervously as he paced toward the cage.

"The problem is that for all we know, trying to remove it might cause the poison to be released," Theo admitted.

Turner's head bobbed forward, "Dear God, what are we supposed to do?"

"We've talked about it at length. Because of how advanced this technology is, we feel it's necessary to remove the last joint of her finger. It's the only way we can ensure her safety," Ned revealed reluctantly.

"What," Turner said incredulously as he glanced at his wife.

"You know how much I love her," Theo said meaningfully. "I wouldn't suggest such a thing if I thought there was another safe way to do this."

Turner swallowed hard as he locked glances with Theo. He knew the man was right, but he also knew that his wife was pregnant again. Would the trauma be harmful to the child? He fretted? Nevertheless, if they didn't do it, both mother and child could be lost.

Sighing, he looked to see if Kenny seemed frightened. She tried to smile as she cocked her head to one side, but couldn't quite pull it off. It appeared; she was resigned to what must happen.

"Just do it quickly and get it over with," she encouraged then.

Miguel reached Lily a small black bag. "I brought the items Theo requested, Novocain, a sterile syringe and the bone cutter."

Turner noticed that his wife winced briefly before getting control of her expression. She always tried to be so brave, he thought with fondness.

"I'm going in with you," he said quietly to his sister.

Lily looked at him quickly, "Are you sure you want to do that?"

"I'm sure," he answered confidently.

Pulling a sympathetic expression his sister gave a quick nod, "Alright, let's get this over with."

Stepping inside the Faraday cage, Turner pulled Kenny into his arms and hugged her close. "I love you," he whispered as Lily prepared the injection.

"You'll feel a little stick now," Lily said as she administered the shot.

"Is it supposed to burn," Kenny asked and gripped the back of Turner's jacket tightly.

"No," Lily assured, "My God," she gasped sounding horrified. "The end of her finger is turning red."

"They must know what we're up to, and have released the poison," Theo surmised. "Do it quickly."

"The Novocain won't have taken effect, Kenny. You're going to feel every bit of this," Lily said apologetically.

"Just do it," Kenny insisted desperately.

Turner felt as if his heart had leapt up into his throat. He hugged his wife tightly to him. And then, buried her face in the crook of his neck, so she wouldn't see any of it.

He heard the snipping sound, and felt Kenny's body stiffened. Her agonized scream was so loud that it seemed to echo throughout the forest surrounding the cabin. Tears flooded Turner's eyes.

"I'm so sorry sweetheart," he whispered in her ear.

2

"How is she doing," Theo questioned with apprehension as Lily returned from bandaging Kenny's hand. All the members of the team were seated around the dining table enjoying a wonderful breakfast made by the estate's head cook, Maria. Three days ago, they arrived at Miguel Torres' vineyard in Talca, Chile. Since then they'd done little else but sleep and eat.

"She's doing pretty well," Lily assured. "She refuses to take anything for the pain because of the baby." Flashing a look of irritation at Turner, she added, "She shouldn't have to worry about that though, now should she?"

Turner felt responsible for every second of pain his wife suffered. Blinking, trying to abate an emotional display, he sighed as he left the table and started to exit the room.

"You shouldn't blame him," he heard his wife saying gently. "He told me what you said about how long we should wait after a miscarriage to get pregnant again. We don't have time to do things as if we weren't hurtling toward the finish line. I've always dreamed of having a baby of my own, Lily. I wanted to feel the baby move, and have at least the possibility of giving birth in the time remaining."

"I'm sorry," Lily apologized quickly, sounding contrite. "It's just that I keep hearing your tortured scream, and I feel guilty because I'm the one who caused it."

Turner had wondered why Lily, who was normally so optimistic and upbeat, had been barking and growling at everyone since that night. Feeling compassion for her, he turned around. Going straight to her, he hugged her close.

"You saved the life of two people that night," He encouraged, "You have nothing to feel guilty about."

"That's right," Kenny agreed and sighed sadly. "If it's anyone's fault, it's mine," she said mindfully. "I'd taken my wedding ring off and placed it on the night stand by the bed. I was shaking so hard after that swim to Elijah's boat. When I gripped the covers to pull them up around my neck, my ring tore a place in the sheet. If I hadn't gone back in for it, none of this would ever have happened."

"I wondered why you went back," Theo admitted quietly.

Spreading her hands in a helpless fashion, she shook her head. "You'd gone to so much trouble to get the rings after my folks died. They were the only things I had left of them," she said and began to sob, "But look at what my selfishness has caused. I lost our baby and put all of you through hell the last five months. I'm so sorry..." covering her face with her hands she wept bitterly.

Giving his sister a sad smile, Turner released her and went to his wife. Pulling her into his arms he gently rubbed her back.

"Hind sight is always 20/20," Theo said then with compassion, "Only God can know the end from the beginning."

"Besides, you don't know what would have happened," Lex interjected. "They seemed determined to experiment with your DNA. It's apparent they thought you were one of the finest physical specimens they'd come across."

"And remember, they were trying to abduct you the night we caught up with you," Theo said then. "I think they had plans for you from the beginning."

Turner watched Kenny's reaction. She frowned as if the thought troubled her.

"We've received a private message from friends in Australia who spoke of something similar happening there in the outback. The group they were hunting were annihilated," Ned said solemnly.

"I think these were just test runs, to see how their super soldiers performed," Cindy added.

"I agree and I don't think they accept defeat gracefully," Theo said thoughtfully. "I'm pretty sure that's why they came after us with such vengeance."

"Could that be the reason we saw the UFO over Panama City?" Lily questioned, "Did they plan to take Kenny that night all along?"

Theo's brows rose thoughtfully, "It could very well be. Governments worldwide are in a race to create super soldiers and killer robots before their competitor does. They'll do anything to be the one who comes out on top, even sell their souls to the devil."

"But, there's something I just don't understand," Kenny broke in. "We weren't being hunted by either of those things. They seemed to be regular human beings."

"They were human, but there was nothing regular about them. Has Turner ever spoken to you about the black awakening," Theo quizzed?

"I asked her if she'd ever heard about it. However, that was just before she received the warning from the Lord to leave the boat."

"It's a very long and involved subject, you might want to research it online when you get a chance." Theo suggested.

"Alright," Kenny agreed, "Speaking of boats, do you think Elijah will be coming back to join us?"

"He said the insurance company was giving him some grief over replacing his yacht. I guess they're trying to claim it was an act of God. Even so, he feels confident that he'll be able to rejoin us in the very near future." Theo explained.

Kenny smiled, "I'm glad; he seems in need of a family. Besides, I worry about him being in the states the way they're persecuting Christians."

"Yeah," Theo agreed, "me, too; however, I believe the man is wise enough to keep that to himself."

"Since I haven't been able to do very much the last few days, I've been watching videos with Cindy online about what's happening in the states. I can hardly recognize it anymore," Kenny said with sadness.

"I know, sweetie, but that's what happens when you kick God out, evil comes flooding in. If the president persists in his attempts to divide the land of Israel. There is something much worse in store for America," Theo announced ominously.

"The day the twin towers came down in New York, that was a warning for the US to change its ways and come back to God," Turner declared. "For a brief time, people sought the Lord and the churches were filled. Nevertheless, it wasn't long before they were back to embracing evil."

"We've slowly been desensitized to what evil is, through board games, video games, TV, music and movies. Some of the most popular forms of entertainment have glamorized witchcraft, vampires and demons. And, we hear about and see so much violence on the news that we hardly pay attention to it anymore. Remember where the Bible says to beware of calling good evil and evil good?" Theo inquired.

"Yes, I remember," Kenny acknowledged. "I also remember when God told Cain that the innocent blood of his brother Able cried out to him from the ground."

Theo pulled a face, "Yes; America has much to repent for, if only she would."

"Sweetheart, why don't you sit down and eat something. You've eaten very little since we arrived," Turner beseeched his wife.

"I am hungry," Kenny admitted and followed as her husband pulled out a chair for her.

Turner watched as she took several sausage patties and filled the rest of her plate with caramelized onions and peppers. He filled her cup with coffee and reached her a pitcher of cream.

"Thank you, this smells wonderful," she cooed and sipped her coffee.

"Ten being the highest and zero the lowest, what is your pain level," Lily said then.

Blinking Kenny answered, "I suppose I'd have to say about a six."

"I know you don't want any pain meds. However, I could give you an injection near the site that would help," Lily offered.

"I'll keep it in mind, perhaps later," Kenny replied as she attempted to cut up the patties on her plate. She was obviously finding it awkward due to the bandages on her left hand.

"Do you want any help with that," Turner asked when he saw that she was having a little trouble.

"Sure," she said and pushed her plate to him. And then seeming thoughtful she said to her uncle, "Do you think, now that I'm maimed I'll be less desirable to those critters?"

Pursing his lips, he shrugged his shoulders, "One could only hope that's the case."

Wanting to change the subject Turner inquired, "So what do you think of this little hideaway that we built?"

She looked at him quickly seemingly amazed, "You guys built this?"

"Yes," he said and smiled, "it's called a Binishell. It only took about six weeks, and that includes the interior design."

"Are you serious," she said with awe, "I've been wandering around this place admiring how beautiful and unusual it is. How did you do it?"

"We decided on the resort design," Theo spoke up then. "That way, because Miguel was so gracious as to let us build on his property; he could use it to rent out rooms to travelers and make a profit. And then, when we needed it we could have the place to ourselves."

"First, we built a wooden form around what would be the base of the building," Lex said then. "We leveled the ground and placed an air bladder, covered with rebar and about a ton of cement inside. When the concrete begins to set, an air pump fills the bladder, and concrete domes magically rise from the earth. After about an hour, the concrete has hardened and the bladder is deflated and removed for reuse. It was absolutely amazing how quickly it went up after all the prep work was done."

"Yeah it was so cool," Cindy agreed.

"I got to spray the grass seed on the outside while everyone else went to work on the inside," Theo said then and smiled.

"I noticed that even from a very short distance away, if you didn't know this building was here, you'd never guess," Kenny said with amazement. "With the grass covering, it's virtually veiled from sight."

"That was the plan," Turner acknowledged. "We only had to remove about three trees, but could leave the rest of the surrounding forest intact. This place is invisible from the air."

"I'll have a new appreciation for it as I go exploring," Kenny said and smiled at the members of the team.

"Didn't know we were so talented, huh," Ned beamed.

"I knew you were talented," Kenny assured. "It just never occurred to me; that construction was one of those abilities."

"Cindy, Ned and Lily designed the interior, Theo, Lex and I made runs into town to pick up supplies. Lex's father was a carpenter, and he is responsible for all the woodwork in the place. It was a lot of fun to watch the whole thing coming together," Turner explained.

"A single Binishell dome can be put up rather quickly and only costs about $3700. It's an excellent way to provide shelter for those living in an area devastated by disaster." Theo explained.

"How did you learn about this," Kenny asked then.

"Theo paid to have one hundred of the Binishell domes' built in Thailand after the Indian Ocean earthquake and tsunami. He heard about them from Franklin Graham, head of Samaritan's Purse," Turner enlightened.

"Wow, that was so wonderful of you to do that, and generous," Kenny said seemingly amazed.

"Being a full professor, I made over a hundred grand a year," Theo confessed. "I had no children to lavish my money on, nor a wife for most of my teaching years. I began tithing after I was saved, and the lord has been good to me."

"What is tithing," Kenny inquired and sipped her coffee.

"It's when you give the first ten percent of your increase to the Lord," Turner explained.

Studying her husband's face, she said, "I'm not making any wage, so how can I tithe?"

Turner's smile was instantaneous, "You don't need to worry about it. Theo and I have written several books on the information we've uncovered over the years. I tithe from the income we get from royalties. Besides, you give 100% of your time to make sure your uncle can get the Word out through his videos."

His wife smiled at him, and he couldn't help but feel like the luckiest man in the world.

3

The weather in Talca in September was comparable to Seattle, low seventies or upper sixties. It was nice; Kenny thought and sighed contentedly as she watched Turner, Lex and Lily leaving to help in the vineyard. Theo explained earlier that it was part of the deal when they needed to stay, they would help with the work.

She couldn't help wondering though if working with the grapes didn't remind Turner and Lily of their mother's alcoholism. Did it bring back all the pain associated with that time of life? She questioned.

For herself, she knew that every time she would catch sight of her wedding ring it evoked a memory. It took her right back to the moment; she'd lost the baby. A fine line of moisture rose in her eyes and she sighed.

"Forgive me, Father," she whispered, feeling solely responsible for the loss of their child.

In her spirit, it was like she heard the Lord speaking softly to her. “She’s with me; I'm taking good care of her.”

“It was a girl,” she whispered; her voice choked with emotion. “I know that she could be in no safer or better place. Thank you, Father,” she said with gratitude as tears streaked down her cheeks.

“Forgive yourself, there is much left for you to do,” He said then.

Wiping her cheeks, she considered what the Father had said. If there were a lot left for them to accomplish, could there be time for her to deliver the child she carried now? She thought with anticipation.

“Are you okay,” Theo inquired from close behind her.

Turning, she witnessed his look of concern. Smiling, she wiped her face and then hugged his neck. “I’m alright,” she assured, “our baby girl is safe with the Lord. He told me I needed to forgive myself because we have a lot to accomplish yet.”

Pulling back his gray eyes studied her questioningly. He adjusted his wire-rimmed glasses, “Sometimes that’s an awful hard thing to do, forgiving ourselves,” he said thoughtfully.

Pulling a face, she nodded her head. “Yes, I know the Father is right. Nevertheless, I feel that if I walk around as if I did nothing wrong, I would be betraying the baby somehow." She confessed knowing she hadn't expressed herself well.

"I understand sweetheart," he said giving her a sad smile. "I beat myself up for a long time after Sophie divorced me. It was primarily my fault. I didn't give her enough of me or my time. I don't think I ever told her just how much she meant to me. I spent months away on digs in faraway lands trying to make an important find so I could make a name for myself, when I returned; I threw myself into my work, and tried to impress the university by publishing my findings."

Kenny gave her uncle a sympathetic smile. "I guess we all screw up, huh?"

"Exactly," he agreed quickly. "Jesus died on the cross to cover every sin, mistake or screw up; we'd ever make." Theo blinked thoughtfully, "Reminds me of a song; Jesus paid it all, all to him; I owe. Sin had left a crimson stain; He washed it white as snow.

"I love the first verse of that song; I hear the savior say, thy strength indeed is small, Child of weakness, watch and pray, find in me thine all in all."

"That's beautiful," Kenny smiled, "It's been a while since I've heard you sing. I miss it. Theo..." she began not quite knowing how to apologize.

"What is it, dear," he inquired studying her carefully.

"I truly regret the way I spoke to you in the van that first night you found me. I had no right to focus all the hurt; I felt at losing my family on you. I'm ashamed of myself for treating you so disrespectfully." Kenny hugged her uncle in an effort to hide the high emotion she felt.

He gently rubbed her back, "I forgive you, sweetheart. Now it's time for you to forgive yourself. We must stop looking back, with sadness. Our past failures are a tool that Satan uses to keep us from moving forward and doing our best for the Lord. We have a glorious future straight ahead of us, when Jesus calls us home, let's focus on that."

"I forgive myself," she said tearfully as she pulled back so she could wipe her face. "I pray the Holy Spirit will help me to keep my eyes on Jesus."

"He will," Theo assured, "hey, why don't you come and sit in while I do my YouTube video?"

Smiling then Kenny nodded, "I'd love that, what are you going to talk about today?"

"I intend to link current events with Bible prophecy. Things are accelerating so quickly now; it's very hard to keep up. Basically, I hope to get reacquainted with my audience. Between being held prisoner in the FEMA camp for six months, and then chased for the last four, I haven't done many new programs. I'm not sure anyone will remember who I am," Theo said and pulled a face.

"I imagine your listeners have kept you in their prayers and will be overjoyed to hear that you're alright." Kenny said with confidence. "It was a while since Elijah had heard a current program, and he knew exactly who you were."

Brightening Theo said then, "By the way, I had a call from Mr. James. He is sailing his new vessel down the coast of South America as we speak. We should see him in a few days."

"I like him," she said and smiled, "he's like a big teddy bear."

"Yes," Theo agreed, "he's become a good friend. When the meteorite demolished his yacht, his only concern was for you, the man never once complained about his loss."

"I'm thankful the insurance company came through and replaced his ship. He's suffered a great deal of forfeiture already."

"We're ready for you," Ned said as both, he and Cindy approached them. "We've been replaying some of your most popular programs during the times when we couldn't put out a new one. I'm sure that your subscribers will be really glad to learn that you're alright and back to doing videos."

"Let's do it," Theo encouraged, as he grasped Kenny's hand.

He led her to the computer room where Ned had a camera set up. Taking his seat, he motioned for her to sit near Cindy, who would be working the computer.

"Do I look presentable; I didn't think to check out my appearance in the mirror."

"You're very handsome," Kenny assured him.

He smiled as if he appreciated her words, but couldn't quite believe it. And then turning thoughtful, he appeared to be deciding what to say.

"Ready in five, four, three, two and you're on," Ned counted it down for him.

"Welcome to, End Times Unfolding. I am your host Dr. Theo Braum," He said and drew a deep breath. "It's been quite a while since we were able to bring you a current broadcast. The last ten months have been very trying times indeed.

"I was abducted and thrown into a prisoner FEMA camp in the US for six months. My crime, sharing the gospel of Christ and warning believers of what is shortly going to come to pass. The whole reason I began doing videos was because I knew that possessing the truth would keep believers safe in Christ when the great deception is revealed. Before I was taken, I'd made videos about the presence of these camps on American soil. Now I can tell you personally that they're much worse than I ever imagined.

"I met pastor's there that I knew personally. I also got to know people who were members of my online ministry." Theo sighed and blinked thoughtfully before going on.

Kenny often wondered what had happened to him while he was held captive. She'd never asked because she didn't wish to cause him the pain of having to relive those memories.

"They demanded that we renounce Jesus and willingly allow them to place an RFID chip, in our right hand. If we didn't we were punished in some way. Most of the people were there because of their love of Christ. They knew well that accepting the mark and denying Jesus would dam their souls to an eternal hell, understandably they refused. Sometimes they would lock us up in a box so small that you couldn't move, for days on end. At other times, they would literally beat us with canes, or hit us with stun guns. Water and food deprivation were other tactics they employed.

"They tried to strip you of all hope by telling you they'd taken all your remaining relative's captive as well. Alternatively," he struggled for several moments, "as in my case they killed most of my family members."

A rebellious tear slid down his face, and he quickly swiped it away. "Even in this they did not win for I have the comfort of knowing that my family is saved and born again. I will see them all in the very near future. As my listeners know we are living in the fleeting seconds of time.

"Soon we will see the face of Jesus. I am reminded of Psalm 9:13. Have mercy upon me, O Lord; consider my trouble which I suffer of them that hate me, thou that liftest me up from the gates of death. Romans 8:18 also comes to mind, For I reckon that the sufferings of this present time are not worthy to be compared with the glory which shall be revealed in us.

"While I was a prisoner, I found myself repeating 1 Peter 2:20 and 21. For what glory is it, if, when ye be buffeted for your faults, ye shall take it patiently? but if, when ye do well, and suffer for it, ye take it patiently, this is acceptable with God. For even hereunto were ye called: because Christ also suffered for us, leaving us an example, that ye should follow his steps.

"Before my team could extract me from that place, I was literally at death's door on numerous occasions. It was in those times that I understood what the apostle Paul meant when he was torn between wanting to go and wanting to stay. I knew if I just let go that I could step into the arms of my Savior. My struggles would at last be over.

"Even so, I knew I had more to do. For this reason, I held onto the life my God had given me," Theo said and briefly smiled at her. "I'm glad I did."

Kenny silently prayed he wouldn't ask her to go on camera. For all they knew, the people pursuing them might have assumed she was dead. If that was the case, she'd like to keep it that way. It might mean fewer dangers for the rest of the team. Thankfully, Theo turned back to the camera without saying anything about her.

"So much has happened since we were last together, I hardly know where to start," he said blinking thoughtfully. "Alliances have been formed in the middle east between Russia, China and Iran. If you've never read Isaiah 17, Psalms 83 or Ezekiel 38 and 39, now is the time to do it. The European Union super state has formed its own army.

"Pray for the peace of Jerusalem," he whispered. "Her enemies surround her and are salivating over the thought of her soon demise."

Kenny listened, enthralled as her uncle pulled world events together with Bible prophecy. Attentive to his every word, she realized there was so much she didn't know. It had always amazed her that the greater the level of knowledge you attained, the more you realized that you knew very little in the scheme of things.

4

Kenny had discovered a bench out behind the Binishell, that was secluded under the low-hanging branches of a cherry tree. While she loved every member of the team, there were times when she just wanted to be alone with her own thoughts. This was one of those times.

When her uncle finished filming his YouTube video, he accompanied Cindy and Ned to the fields to help with the grape harvest. Feeling bored because they wouldn't let her help in the work, she decided to watch several videos about the Black Awakening.

Now as she sat in this beautiful setting, she felt troubled by what she'd learned. Theo implied that the people who chased them for five months were a part of this awakening. Some of them were victims of Satanic Ritual Abuse, and were referred to as SRAs. Others had their psyche fractured with mind-altering drugs and mind control.

It didn't sound to her as if these poor people had much of a choice in their actions. How many of them had she shot and killed over the past several months? Silently she knew that she couldn't even venture a guess. It was true that they didn't leave them with many other options; they'd hunted them down like rabid dogs. At the time, she was convinced they were not super soldiers. However, she thought that some of them were possibly hybrids, or else Artificial Intelligence.

Her emotions were conflicted. Once again, she wondered how long she could continue the fight if in doing so she became less human herself. Sighing, she realized she'd been staring at the ground for the last twenty minutes. Spreading her hands out over her growing waistline, she knew with a certainty that she would fight to the death for the life of their child.

"There you are," Turner said sounding relieved, "I've been looking all over for you."

"Sorry," she answered thoughtfully, "I needed a quiet place to think."

"Anything wrong," he inquired studying her carefully.

Glancing at her husband, she took a deep breath before answering. "I finally looked into what the Black Awakening is."

He gave a knowing nod of his head, "Pretty scary stuff, isn't it?"

"Yes, it is," she answered quietly before meeting his glance once more. "And the most chilling part of all is that it doesn't sound as if these people had any choice in what was done to them."

"For the most part, it doesn't seem so," Turner granted. "Nevertheless, make no mistake about it, they're just as deadly as all the rest. If their designation is to murder and kill, you have few options if they come after you."

"I know," she responded regretfully, "it just seems that they are broken."

Turner gently clasped her right hand in his. "There are pastors, which are working with them in an effort to bring them out of that life and to a saving knowledge of Christ."

"Yes," she agreed, "I read about one who has been doing this for thirty years. He also works with law enforcement to teach them about SRA victims. Thank God for the work he's doing."

"Theo believes they must have been activated whenever they got into close proximity with the RFID chip you were tagged with. And," he said and shook his head seemingly confused, "It certainly appeared that way."

"Perhaps the frequency they used to track us gave off a signal that activated the SRAs," Kenny suggested.

Her husband frowned, “Maybe,” he responded quietly. “But that would mean that the angelic and human rebellions have merged, and I don’t like the sound of that.”

“Well,” she sighed, “hopefully; they believe the lethal dose; they put in the chip did its job. And we’ll at least get a bit of a respite before anything else happens.”

Turner glanced at her and smiled before gently putting his hand on her abdomen. Placing his free arm around her back, he pulled her close and kissed her. “I love you,” he whispered and pressed his forehead against hers.

“Even though I’m now disfigured,” she said curious how he felt about the change in her.

Pulling back his turquoise glance washed over her face, “Honey, you haven’t seriously been concerned about that, have you?”

Seeing the mixture of love and anxiety in his eyes, she felt bad for having said it. Giving a small shake of her head, she whispered, “No.”

His eyes closed with relief as he hugged her near once more. “The world has gone crazy,” he whispered by her ear. “I truly don’t know how much longer things can go on this way. I want you to promise me that no matter what happens, you will fight to go on as long as possible.”

Pulling back, she studied his face, “You know I will, and I expect the same from you.”

His expression warmed slightly, "You should know by now that I will fight with every ounce of strength I possess to remain at your side for as long as possible."

"Why do you sound as if you think something will happen to you," Kenny questioned with a concerned frown.

Blinking, he appeared to be gathering his thoughts. "I don't know how to explain it except to say that in my spirit, I feel a major kingdom shift has taken place. Remember Matthew 24:22, except those days should be shortened, there should be no flesh saved?"

"Yes, I remember," Kenny assured him.

"This verse came to me the other day and ever since, the words 'those days' keep repeating in my mind. I feel that the Holy Spirit is trying to tell me we've stepped over into an extremely perilous period of time."

Kenny pulled in a deep breath and released it slowly. Thinking about this past year she found it hard to believe that things could get much worse. However, she recalled Luke 21:26; Men's hearts failing them for fear, and for looking after those things which are coming on the earth: for the powers of heaven shall be shaken.

In fact, all of chapter 21 warned of the things coming upon the earth. "Well," She said quietly, "I read that men have desired to live to see Jesus call up the church. I heard it referred to as the desire of the ages. Little did we know what these days would look like. Still, to hear the trumpet sound and catch the Lord's voice calling us homeward, would be worth any amount of persecution we must face."

Turner smiled, "Yes," he agreed softly, "I look forward to knowing our two babies in heaven."

Just at that moment Kenny felt a distinct thump against her belly where her husband's hand rested. "Did you feel that," she asked excitedly.

"I did," Turner acknowledged bearing a wide smile, "Is this the first time you've felt the baby move?"

"It is," she assured him as two more thumps followed quickly.

Sheer delight lit her husband's turquoise eyes. Leaning down he gently kissed her stomach. And then, he kissed her lips. "Thank you," he whispered against her mouth. "The joy of this moment will carry me through whatever else we may face."

Their bliss lasted precious few seconds before they heard what sounded like a large explosion. Lightning forks stabbed to the earth out of a cloudless sky. The next sound they heard was of a woman alternately screaming and crying.

Turner's eyes grew large as saucers as he launched to his feet. "That's Lily," he announced as he grabbed Kenny's hand, and they ran inside the Binishell. "You stay here," he instructed as he drew the handgun from the holster under his left arm. "Stay away from the windows or anything that uses electricity," he shouted back over his shoulder before running out the door toward the vineyard.

Kenny prayed hard as she waited for the team members to return.

Turner could hardly believe his eyes as he ran toward the sound of his sister's screams. A large tree was split down the middle. Smoldering chunks of it lay all over the ground, as well as several bodies. Scanning as he hurried he realized that so far, they were men Miguel hired to bring in the crop.

When he entered the row where the team had been working he found Lily frantically giving Lex CPR.

"Let me take over," he insisted as he returned his weapon to its holster, and dropped to his knees beside his old friend.

Exhausted Lily nodded and let him do it. Picking up his hand, she felt for his pulse. "Hold up for a second," she said breathlessly and concentrated. After a few seconds, she shook her head, saying tearfully, "I can't find it, oh God please, don't let him die."

Turner resumed CPR; he'd known for quite some time that Lex and Lily cared for each other. He was never certain why they hadn't acted on their feelings for one another. Nevertheless, the man wasn't going to die, not if he could help it. Desperate at his lack of progress, Turner pounded his fist down in the middle of Lex's chest, and raised his arm to do it again.

Immediately, his eyes flew open as he began to suck in air. Turning him on his side Lily patted his back sharply. "Thank God, are you all right," she demanded emotionally.

"I get struck by lightning, and your brother beats the crap out of me," he said shaking his head. And then, attempting a smile Lex said, "I'm just happy to be alive. Is everyone else alright?"

Fat tears rolled down Lily's cheek as she shook her head, "Cindy...didn't make it," she announced and dissolved into tears.

"Where is she," Turner asked as he jumped to his feet.

"The next row, Theo and Ned are with her," she managed.

Stepping into the next row, he saw Ned on his knees next to Cindy's body. He could hear him weeping quietly. Theo met his glance, his cheeks wet with tears. Pulling in a deep breath to steady himself, Turner went to stand beside the young computer whiz.

The sight that met his eyes nearly sickened him. Cindy's face and arms were badly charred; she was hardly recognizable. And she'd been impaled right through her chest by a sharp piece from a tree, that was about the size of a baseball bat. Tears burned in the back of his eyes. She was so young; he thought as he turned away and allowed his emotions free reign.

Lex and Lily joined them, and Turner quickly swiped at the moisture on his face.

"Oh, my God," Lex spoke in a pained whisper.

"Cindy is already with our Lord," Theo said quietly. "Does she have family that we should contact?"

Ned shook his head, "She lived in multiple foster homes until she was eighteen. Cindy rarely spoke about it, and I got the feeling; she wasn't very close with any of them."

"We can bury her body near the Binishell," Theo suggested, "if that's alright with everyone."

"Do you have any objection to that, Ned," Turner asked with compassion.

Getting to his feet, he shook his head as he wiped the tears from his cheeks. "It really doesn't matter, like Theo said she's with the Lord."

"I'll go and get a sheet to wrap her in," Lily said then, "I'll be right back."

"Why don't the rest of you step away while I remove the piece of wood from her chest," Turner suggested.

Theo nodded and put his arm around Ned's shoulder and directed him away from the area.

Lex stubbornly stayed, "I'm not going anywhere; you might need my help."

Looking at his friend, Turner pulled in a long slow breath. He wanted to be steady for the job that lay before him.

5

Kenny laid awake most of the night trying not to disturb her husband. Scenes from her time spent with Cindy, kept flashing through her mind preventing her from getting to sleep. She loved the way Cindy's eyes would dance with laughter when something tickled her. She would be sorely missed. All the members of the team were greatly saddened at her loss.

Thinking about the impromptu funeral they'd held for her, Kenny recalled her uncle's words. "I suppose it was unrealistic to expect that we would all be together when Jesus called us home. Even so, I was taken aback at this loss. I will miss her sweet smile as well as the sound of her laughter."

The timing of this loss did seem strange. Here they were in a place of beauty and quiet, with no one pursuing them. She'd lived through the attack of the hybrids on the island and the meteorites in Panama City. That wasn't even mentioning the battle at the abandoned military base. Nor did it take into account the last five months where they'd run for their lives.

On a beautiful day with a cloudless sky in southern Chili, she'd met her demise through a freak lightning storm. What were the chances of that? She wondered sadly.

Kenny recalled walking to the entrance of the Binishell with Cindy as she was leaving to work in the fields that day. The girl drew in a deep breath of fresh air. "I love this place," she said with fervor, "I wish I could stay here forever."

A tear slid down Kenny's cheek as she realized that she'd gotten her wish. Her body at least would remain until the Lord called her home. Slipping quietly out from beneath the sheet, she grabbed her robe and silently left the room.

Covering her mouth with her hand she went immediately outside. Only then did she allow herself to weep in earnest. The others had known Cindy much longer than she had. Kenny didn't want to cause them any further sorrow.

And then, she became aware she was hearing a strange noise. The sky was just beginning to lighten. Tying the belt of her robe, she wiped her face and walked out a little way to see if she could determine what it was. It sounded like someone was applying an echo machine, an instrument that musicians used to alter electronically the sound of their voice, to the screech of a very large bird. It was like nothing she'd ever heard before. It was extremely loud and seemed to be coming at her from all directions.

The hair on her arms stood straight up as goose bumps washed down over her body. Hearing footsteps behind her, she whipped around to find Turner and the others coming outside. Putting her hand to her chest, she said emphatically, "Oh my God, you scared me."

"Sorry, honey," Turner apologized as he came to stand beside her. "I couldn't find you, and we heard that sound, what is it?"

"I have no idea," she answered sounding mystified, "It's so eerie."

"There are numerous videos online of strange unexplainable sounds being heard all over the world." Theo said then as he searched the sky.

"It sounds like its surrounding us," Lily said anxiously, "Could they be doing construction in the area?"

"Not at this hour," Theo assured, "besides; Miguel owns the land for miles in all directions. He wouldn't allow it."

They could see across the way that warm yellow lights were coming on up at the estate house and in the worker's cabins. The next thing they heard was, many people speaking rapidly in Spanish. Their voices quieted as the noise grew louder once again. It was obvious from the shadows moving about in the pre-dawn light that everyone was curious about the origin of that sound.

"Is it anything to be fearful of," Kenny inquired as she moved closer to her husband.

"Predicated on the information I have, I would say no," Theo said then. "Nevertheless, I've got to admit that it reminds me of the sound the Velociraptor's made in the movie Jurassic Park. And, those babies were lethal because they would attack in herds."

Kenny turned and studied her uncle's face, "Could the Watchers do that?"

Blinking thoughtfully, his expression sobered as if he hadn't considered that possibility before. "If they set their mind to it, I believe they could."

That was not exactly the answer Kenny was hoping for. "I thought the extinction event that took the dinosaurs out was an asteroid strike, wouldn't that have happened long before the Watchers came down to the earth?"

"The Bible not only refers to the evil the Watchers wrought in Noah's day, it also speaks of dinosaurs in the book of Job," Ned interjected. "In the original Hebrew, there were three animals listed that we no longer recognize today. As close as we can get using Roman characters they were;

tanniyn, behemoth and livyathan. Tanniyn is used twenty-eight times in the Bible and is normally translated dragon. However, it can also be translated as serpent, dinosaur, great creature and reptile. So, you see, it's just as likely that the cannibalistic giants, followed by the great flood, are the extinction events that brought about their demise."

Stunned, Kenny's glance shifted toward the sky. The twinkling stars were beginning to fade from view. Men's hearts failing them for fear, and for looking after those things which are coming on the earth: for the powers of heaven shall be shaken. This verse from Luke 21:26 came to mind.

Could the return of dinosaurs be in part, what causes men's hearts to fail? She considered. It seemed so outrageous that she was about to dismiss the idea. And then, she recalled the enormous UFO hovering silently over Panama City, and her Nephilim captors cloning an entire army of super soldiers from her blood. In light of those events, bringing the dinosaurs back didn't seem so impossible.

"How likely is it that we could see a return of the dinosaurs," Kenny said quietly.

"I don't know," Theo admitted, "to be honest it hadn't occurred to me before that it was even a possibility."

The sound became so ear piercingly loud that they had to plug their ears with their fingers. It lasted for about two minutes and then stopped unexplainably.

"I hope that's the end of that," Lex said with feeling.

"Yeah," Theo agreed, "Let's go back inside and make some coffee..." his cell phone rang before he could finish. "Hey, Miguel," he said as he motioned for them to go ahead.

"I'll get the coffee going," Lily volunteered as she headed for the kitchen.

"Ned and I can get breakfast," Lex offered, "is that okay with you," he asked the computer whiz.

Shrugging he said, "That's fine, but I only know how to make pancakes."

"Sounds good," Turner said with a smile.

Since Cindy's untimely death, everyone had been trying to keep Ned occupied. From what Kenny understood they were not in love with each other; however, they were the best of friends.

Heading for their bedroom, Kenny made quick work of getting dressed. She couldn't shake the feeling that something was wrong. Of course, it could be all that talk of dinosaurs or just that bazaar sound coming out of nowhere. She realized with a sigh that it could also simply be due to the loss of their friend.

She didn't sleep very well the past two nights since the funeral. That probably had something to do with it as well. The world was turned upside down and backwards; she knew that it could be due to any number of things.

"You're awfully quiet," Turner observed as he walked toward her.

Looking at her husband, she pulled a face, "I know. Maybe it's just hormonal changes, but I feel out of sorts, like something is off."

Her husband's black brows rose high on his forehead. "It could be due to many of the things we've experienced lately," he said and sighed. "It's best just to give those sorts of feelings to the Lord."

"Since accepting Jesus as my savior, I really haven't been worried about much of anything. It seemed to come on me after hearing that strange sound," she explained as she brushed out her long blond hair.

Turner smiled at her compassionately in the mirror and gently wrapped his arms around her waist. "We've been through so much..." he began but stopped at hearing a knock at their door.

"I need to speak to everyone right away," Theo spoke loudly.

"We'll be right there," Turner assured and appeared concerned. They went immediately in search of her uncle and found him in the kitchen with the others.

“We need to pack up and be ready to leave in an hour,” he informed bluntly.

“Is something wrong, Boss,” Lex inquired.

“Miguel is our friend, but he’s also a business man who must make a profit from his winery.” Theo said and sighed. “Last night they found a huge sinkhole at the northwest corner of his vineyard. The worker’s he hired to bring in the crop are very superstitious. They believe we are bringing them bad luck.

“In the few days since we arrived here many bad and strange things have happened. Remember, they lost three of their own to the lightning strikes. They’ve given Miguel an ultimatum; either we leave or they will. He would be hard-pressed to find enough men to harvest the grapes this late in the season, especially when they learn why these men refuse to do the job.”

“Persona non-grata, huh,” Ned said sounding hurt.

Theo adjusted his wire-rimmed glasses giving a shake of his head. “Miguel hated to tell me how the workers were feeling; he truly did. Remember, when we needed his help, he was there for us. I don’t know what would have happened to us if he hadn’t built and delivered the Faraday cage.”

"Where will we go," Kenny inquired quietly.

Smiling, her uncle glanced at her, "I called Elijah to check his progress. He put into a small port in Constitucion late last night. It's about forty-three miles from here. Miguel will drive us there as soon as we've eaten and gathered our things.

Relief flooded her, "It will be good to see him again."

An hour later, after they'd eaten and placed their packed bags out front, they all stood around Cindy's impromptu grave.

"She'd probably never even held a weapon in her hand before, and yet she saved my life," Kenny said sadly. "I will never forget her."

"None of us will," the majority of the others chimed in simultaneously.

"If you listen closely you can hear that mirth filled giggle of hers," Theo said and smiled. "She's undoubtedly having fun with all the things; the Lord held in store for her."

Hot tears flowed down Kenny's cheeks, "I know, and I'm sure she's happy to be with the Lord in heaven. It's just that I miss her terribly, I guess my tears are for myself."

Turner pulled her into his arms, "It won't be long before we are with her again."

6

"Elijah, who is this vision of loveliness," Theo inquired as they boarded the yacht.

Turner thought the girl looked to be around eighteen or twenty. She had a lighter shade of red hair and green eyes. She stood about five feet five and was very slender.

"This is my niece, Emma," he introduced, "she ran a fowl of the law back in the states. I smuggled her out of the country. Her parents were afraid that the government planned to throw her into a FEMA camp."

"What did you do," Ned inquired of her as they all found a seat.

"My uncle told me about your program several years ago," she said addressing Theo. "I found it fascinating when you spoke about the underground cities. I figured they must have surveillance cameras. I made it my goal to hack into their feed, so I could see what was going on down there."

Ned bolted up out of his chair, seemingly flabbergasted. Plowing his fingers back through his messy short dark-brown hair, his brown eyes were wide with wonder. "We've been trying to accomplish that for years, are you saying you were successful?"

Smiling she nodded her head, "Yeah, it took me about five years to accomplish it though. They had security like you wouldn't believe."

"Did you hear that, Cindy," he said excitedly as he looked around the room for her. Realizing his blunder Ned's expression instantly sobered, and his eyes fell closed. Giving a quick shake of his head, he bore a deep frown. "I guess I'm used to sharing breakthroughs with her. Sorry..." he apologized and sat back down in his chair.

Turner's heart went out to the young man. That very morning he'd barely stopped himself from suggesting that Cindy could show his wife videos about strange noises being heard around the globe.

"Don't beat yourself up," Theo insisted with compassion. "We'd gotten used to having Cindy around. It will take a little time before we no longer look for her to be there."

"Yes," Elijah affirmed sadly, "Theo told me of the loss you suffered, I'm so very sorry."

Ned tried to smile at the captain and gave an appreciative nod of his head. "Thank you," he acknowledged.

Wanting to change the direction the conversation was going, Turner looked to Theo. “Didn’t you say that you thought you were transported between FEMA camps via those underground tunnels?”

Theo’s brows danced on his forehead, and he nodded, “I’m certain of it. I was blindfolded of course, and they bound my hands behind me. Obviously, they didn’t want me to see anything clearly. However, the last time I was moved; I could see the tiniest bit out of the corner of my right eye.

“I was taken aboard what I suspect to be a magneto levitron train. They buckled me in; the train took off. The g-force slammed me back against my seat, and I thought I might be ill. One of the guards seemed to notice I was a little green around the gills. ‘Hang in there, it only takes a few minutes to get from California to Montana in this train,’ he boasted.

Another guard reprimanded him for what he’d told me. The first guard defended himself by saying that it didn’t matter, because I wouldn’t survive the Montana FEMA camp anyway.”

“Did you see any of the critters that reside in the tunnels,” Emma inquired.

“No,” Theo admitted, “I spent very little time there.”

"Did you see any of them," Ned asked skeptically as his eyes narrowed on Elijah's niece.

They watched as she pulled a flash drive from her purse. "I did, and I recorded for nearly an hour before the men in black pulled up outside my parents' home. I hid behind a false door in my closet for six hours while they searched for me. My computer was confiscated, along with several other devices I had.

"They kept the house under constant surveillance for two weeks," she revealed.

"How did you get away," Kenny inquired.

"My mom hired someone to bomb an empty strip mall near our home. As she hoped, all but one of the government vehicles left to investigate. She also arranged for a couple of guys to drag race up our street and to make it look as if they accidentally ran into their vehicle. In the confusion, we could slip out to the alley where a family friend was waiting, and we sped away."

"There isn't much my sister wouldn't do for her family," Elijah interjected. "She's also a fan of your program, so she knows what we're up against."

"Where are your parents now," Kenny asked, "are they somewhere safe?"

The girl's eyebrows rose high as she blinked thoughtfully. "I'm not sure there are any safe places anymore," she said with a note of sadness.

"We were preparing to leave the states when Uncle Elijah contacted us. Once I learned what he'd been up to, and that he was planning to return to your team, I begged him to take me with him. My parents flew on to Europe; they'll contact us when they're settled."

"Can we see what's on the drive," Ned requested and reached out his hand.

"Well," Emma said and raked her teeth across her lower lip. "You're welcome to look at it if you don't think it will rain down a load of trouble on you."

"We won't be watching a live feed. So, I don't see how it could draw attention to us," Ned reassured.

She seemed to be considering what he'd said as she placed the flash drive gingerly in the palm of Ned's hand. "Be careful," she warned ominously.

Turner felt Kenny's hand tighten around his. Glancing at his wife, she appeared apprehensive. Giving her hand a gentle squeeze, he drew her attention, and smiled at her. A smile slowly came to her lovely face. As he glanced around the room at the other members of the team, he found each of them bore the same uneasy expression. Lily leaned closer to Lex, who put his arm around her protectively. Perhaps, Turner thought; either the close call for Lex at Miguel's vineyard or else the reminder that our lives are fragile and could end at a moment's notice, caused them fully to realize their feelings for one another.

"Listen," Theo said drawing their attention, "everyone here knows that you don't get out of this life alive. Until the Lord calls us home, we will do the work he has given us to do."

Ned retrieved his laptop from one of the duffel bags. And then, he placed it on the end of the coffee table where everyone would be able to view the screen. Picking up the drive, he put it in the USB port.

"You'll notice that every so often it appears as if I get kicked out of one terminal only to go to another one of their underground feeds." Emma advised.

"Alright," Ned said as his fingers flew over the keyboard, "let's see what we've got."

The first picture that came up on the screen was a shot of what looked like an empty hallway. The quality was somewhat grainy, even so; you could determine what you were looking at.

Next, they saw a high-ranking military man walking toward the camera. From a door, off to the right-hand side appeared a red-haired giant of a man, who stood nearly twice as tall as the officer. While everyone on Elijah's boat seemed amazed, the officer was not the least bit surprised at his appearance.

"My God," Kenny whispered, "you said that giants were already here, but I guess I didn't want to believe it."

Turner put his arm around her back and pulled her close. "I've had more than one enlisted man tell me of their experiences with giants. One of them was actually in a battle with one in Kandahar Afghanistan before they killed it. The other man was dispatched to fly its remains to a secret location."

Looking back to the screen, Turner was amazed that the giant gave the commanding officer an order. He saluted the Nephilim and hurried away to do his bidding. He could scarcely believe his eyes. The sound quality of the recording wasn't very good, so he couldn't tell what was said. He realized, however, that he really didn't have to hear it to know who was in charge.

His glance found Theo's, "They're in control of our military."

Theo cocked his head to one side, "You're not really surprised, are you?"

Turner's turquoise glance wandered back to the laptop, "Hardly anything surprises me anymore. However, I just never pictured a four-star general behaving like a new recruit."

"You're going to see a lot of strange things from here on out," Theo assured in an uneasy tone.

"This is where it skips to what looks like a lab filled with half human, half animal monstrosities," Emma warned.

"The first image they saw was that of a Centaur. Just like in Greek mythology, he had the head and torso of a human and the body of a horse. He was moving about the lab, checking his notes and giving injections to the myriad of other hideous chimaeras. He seemed to be in command.

"What is that," Kenny whispered as a creature with a lion's body and the head and wings of an eagle came into view.

"That's a griffin," Theo informed sounding flatly amazed at the sight.

A Minotaur, with the head of a bull and the body of a man, brought a stack of files to the centaur. "Put them there," he instructed as he pointed to a file holder on the counter. The Minotaur did as he was told and left the room.

For the next few moments, the centaur worked with a many headed snake and what appeared to be a very young winged dragon. Without warning, the scene changed.

Around a large, table sat several high-ranking leaders from all branches of the military and the government. Interspersed between them were many ghoulish looking entities. Some looked like grays, or what most people referred to as aliens. Others looked like powerful angels with wings. The last group had the bodies of men, but their heads looked reptilian. Their eyes had vertical slits instead of round shaped pupils.

Kenny jumped to her feet announcing emphatically, "They're the ones who held me captive at the military base."

"The reptilians," Turner inquired.

"Yes," she answered ardently and slowly sat back down beside her husband.

"It won't be long now," said an elderly white-haired man as he entered the room. He was donning the same vestments that Catholic priests wore during mass.

"He's almost ready to make his appearance," he continued as he took his place at the podium in the front of the room. Just as he opened his mouth to say more the scene skipped again.

In this room, men in lab coats worked on artificial intelligence on one side. The face of the AI seated in a chair closest to the camera, appeared so lifelike it was scary. The back of its head wasn't yet covered with hair. Its mannerisms were that of a human.

"What is your ultimate goal," the technician asked it after making an adjustment to one of its components.

The female AI winked at him, "I want to be smarter than man and become immortal."

The camera chose that moment to adjust and focus in on what Turner could only describe as the Borg. The Borg was a collection of species that were turned into cybernetic organisms. They functioned as drones in a hive mind called the Collective, or the hive. Cloning chambers like the ones they observed at the abandoned military base also lined the back wall.

In another area of this room, massive machines were being assembled. A lab tech asked a powerfully built robot that stood about ten feet tall, "what do you think of our newest member?" The robot considered the question and answered, "I think he looks weak. He's a poor reflection on the rest of us. We should melt it down and start over."

"He's sentient," Theo whispered, his voice filled with astonishment.

The scene switched again to what appeared to be a gigantic supply room. It looked to house all the essentials for a lengthily underground stay for thousands of people.

"She must have tapped into the feed of one of the D.U.M.B.'s," Ned said then.

"What's that," Emma questioned, seemingly confused by the acronym.

"Deep underground military base," Ned replied absently as he continued to watch the feed.

Suddenly, without warning the recording came to an end.

7

"This is where I had to grab the flash drive and quickly hide in the secret place in my closet that my dad built for me. I knew they would confiscate all my devices. Nevertheless, as long as I had the drive, I had proof of what I'd found," Emma explained.

"The hordes of hell are readying themselves to make their appearance," Theo said ominously. Leaning forward, his expression serious, he looked at Elijah's niece. "Do I have your permission to show this video during my YouTube program tomorrow? I promise I won't mention how I came across it."

The young girl swallowed hard as she glanced at each member of their group. "They came after me with a vengeance," she cautioned. "If you show that, you'll be putting yourself right in their cross hairs."

Theo pulled a humorless smile and sighed, "Sweetheart; we've been in their sights for years. No matter how dangerous, we are indebted to the Lord for the sacrifice that He made for us upon the cross. People need to know what will be coming at them in the very near future.

"Sadly, the church is asleep, for the most part. A lot of them have been lulled into believing the politically-correct rhetoric of the main-stream media. That's why many churches have melded themselves into the Chrislam movement. If they hear the truth and reject it, that's on them. However, I am obliged to present them with the truth. I am a bondservant for Christ."

"Matthew 11:15, He who has ears to hear, let him hear," Kenny recited after listening to their exchange.

She'd always thought it an odd verse. When she was eleven and first read the Bible, she thought how could someone help but hear unless they were deaf. She didn't realize then that it meant possessing a knowledge of the truth so that you could recognize it when you heard it.

"I don't understand how people could believe all this crazy stuff," Emma said with a disheartened sigh. "It seems like the whole world is upside down and backwards. Take, for example, abortion. You'll see women marching and hotly demanding the right to murder their babies. God made women the ones to nurture and care for the children. It seems perfectly logical to me that if after nine months you have a baby, it was a human being all along. So, if you end the pregnancy, you've taken the life of someone God created and loved. Why can't they see that? And that's just one of countless things I could mention."

"This is part of the great deception spoken of in 2 Thessalonians 2," Turner said then. "Now we beseech you, brethren, by the coming of our Lord Jesus Christ, and by our gathering together unto him,

2 That ye be not soon shaken in mind, or be troubled, neither by spirit, nor by word, nor by letter as from us, as that the day of Christ is at hand.

3 Let no man deceive you by any means: for that day, shall not come, except there come a falling away first, and that man of sin be revealed, the son of perdition;

4 Who opposeth and exalteth himself above all that is called God, or that is worshipped; so, that he as God sitteth in the temple of God, shewing himself that he is God.

5 Remember ye not, that, when I was yet with you, I told you these things?

6 And now ye know what withholdeth that he might be revealed in his time.

7 For the mystery of iniquity doth already work: only he who now letteth will let, until he be taken out of the way.

8 And then shall that Wicked be revealed, whom the Lord shall consume with the spirit of his mouth, and shall destroy with the brightness of his coming:

9 Even him, whose coming is after the working of Satan with all power and signs and lying wonders,

10 And with all deceivableness of unrighteousness in them that perish; because they received not the love of the truth, that they might be saved.

11 And for this cause God shall send them strong delusion, that they should believe a lie:

12 That they all might be damned who believed not the truth, but had pleasure in unrighteousness.

13 But we are bound to give thanks always to God for you, brethren beloved of the Lord, because God hath from the beginning chosen you to salvation through sanctification of the Spirit and belief of the truth:

14 Whereunto he called you by our gospel, to the obtaining of the glory of our Lord Jesus Christ.

15 Therefore, brethren, stand fast, and hold the traditions which ye have been taught, whether by word, or our epistle.

16 Now our Lord Jesus Christ himself, and God, even our Father, which hath loved us, and

hath given us everlasting consolation and good hope through grace,

17 Comfort your hearts, and stablish you in every good word and work."

"Amen," the others murmured fervently from around the room.

"Alright," Emma agreed, "you can use the video on your show."

"Thank you," Theo said with appreciation, "This will cause many to want to be saved."

Feeling several hard thumps near her ribs, Kenny straightened and placed her hand over the area.

"Feels like the little guy is doing back flips," she acknowledged, getting to her feet.

"The baby is moving already," Lily said sounding astonished, "Is this the first time?"

"No," Kenny revealed with a sad shake of her head.

"How long have you felt movement," Lily wanted to know.

"I've only felt the baby move one other time," she confessed. "It...was right before the lightning storm at Miguel's vineyard. Of course, I was excited about it and wanted to share the news with everyone. However, given what happened; I didn't really feel the timing was right."

"Can I feel," Theo asked with excitement, "As you know; we couldn't have any children of our own. So, I've never felt a baby move in the womb."

"Of course, you may," Kenny said and put his hand on just the right place. The baby didn't disappoint him.

His smile was instantaneous, "Wow," he whispered as if totally amazed by the experience. "What a miracle child birth is," he said with reverence.

Looking at her, he inquired, "Are you fearful of me releasing the video. I mean, because of the danger, it will most assuredly place us in?"

"I would be lying if I said it didn't give me pause," she admitted. "Even so, I know that no matter what happens from here on out, Turner and I will have two children with us in heaven. No one can take that from us, even if they take our lives."

Her uncle hugged her tight, "I'm so happy that you at least got to feel the baby move. Whether or not there's time for the child to be born, is yet to be seen. I hope so; however, considering how advanced are their evil plans; I believe the Lord will call us home very soon."

Lex got to his feet and looking at Lily, he said, "Could we talk out on the deck?"

Nodding she said, “Sure,” as she took the hand he offered to help her to her feet.

Once they were out of earshot Kenny quizzed, “Do you think he’s going to propose?”

Turner smiled, “I think he is. It seems like his near-death experience has changed his mind about remaining single to the end.”

“I believe it also has to do with how bravely the two of you are facing the dangers of these end times,” Theo ventured. “Despite all you’ve been through, you’re still carrying out the mandate to be fruitful and multiply. It’s encouraging to others that you haven’t dwelt on the loss, rather you look forward to the gathering.”

Turner smiled wistfully; he relished the idea of meeting his children one day soon.

“I hope you don’t mind the interruption, but I have a question,” Emma said then.

“Sure, go ahead,” Theo encouraged.

“In the room with all the dignitaries, a Catholic priest walked in. I noticed none of you seemed particularly surprised by that,” she said and shook her head as if confused.

“Satan is always imitating God. You’ve heard of the holy trinity; the Father, Son and Holy Spirit, I'm sure,” Theo said looking at Emma questioningly.

The girl nodded, “I have,” she acknowledged observing him expectantly.

"Satan's unholy trinity consists of the dragon (Satan), the beast and the false prophet. A lot of people believe that whoever is Pope when the antichrist is revealed, will be a part of that unholy trinity; the false prophet."

"How can that be," she whispered, clearly unable to wrap her mind around the concept.

Cocking his head to one side he inquired with care, "Are you Catholic?"

"No, however, I have many friends who are, and after seeing that I'm worried about them."

"You've never seen any of my programs dealing with the Pope and the great end time deception, have you?"

Blinking, Emma shook her head. "It's only been since I graduated in June that I've had much free time. Before that I had school and homework and all the things that go along with being a senior in high school. When I did have time, I worked on hacking that feed."

"It's understandable; a student looks forward to their senior year. You were right to enjoy it," Theo remarked with a smile.

"There are a multitude of archived programs on Theo's web site," Turner explained gently. "It would probably help you a great deal to go back and watch some of them."

"I will," she agreed easily, "but tell me one thing. You've mentioned the great end time deception; do you know exactly how people will be deceived?"

"In Rome in April 2014, Pope Francis, in his homily in St. Peter's Square announced; soon we will know our new brothers and sisters with whom we will exchange a sign of peace. On that day, there will be wonder...

"There's so much I could say on this topic. I'll try to boil it down; however, the subject is vast, and I could quite literally speak for hours. Soon, the Vatican will announce the arrival of an alien savior. They will convince the masses that we were created by these aliens and seeded on this planet in ages past. They'll say that we should worship them and not God. These aliens are in fact demonic fallen angels."

Turner noticed amusement playing across the girl's expression; it seemed obvious that she thought the very idea preposterous.

Theo adjusted his wire-rimmed glasses and scooted forward in his chair. "You have accepted Jesus as your savior, right?"

"Yes," she nodded, "my whole family said the sinner's prayer with you at the end of one of your programs."

"That's excellent; I'm glad to hear it. The fact that you are saved and belong to the Lord is why this sounds so ridiculous to you. You know the truth. The sad fact is that many have rejected the truth, and so they **will** accept the lie.

"You've just graduated from school, and they pushed evolution down your throat, didn't they?"

"Yes, they did," Emma acknowledged quickly.

"What is coming is unprecedented and the roots of it are founded in Darwinism. Darwinism sets up both an intellectual and spiritual vacuum in people's lives. They begin to wonder, where did it all start then? There are those in academia, science and the exo-politic movement, who are looking for our creators, our progenitors. They've begun to look at ET, and the pan-spermia theory. That's the idea of aliens seeding us on this planet. Darwinism is the paradigm that sets up the coming great deception, because it cuts away at the Christian world view.

"In May of 2014, the Pope said he would baptize aliens. Forty or fifty years ago, if the Pope had made such a declaration, they would have laughed him into derision. Today after years of cultural conditioning, mainly through science fiction, people believe in aliens. And many have seen UFOs for themselves. There are upwards of one hundred and fifty UFO sightings every day.

"Programs like My Favorite Martian and Star Trek from back in the 60s introduced us to alien races from across the galaxy. Remember, Superman was an alien. And then came, War of the Worlds, The X-Files, Transformers, The Visitor, and Species. On and on it goes, the list of films portraying aliens is quite lengthily. You can go to Wikipedia and find it for yourself. And you'll realize why the idea of interacting with aliens no longer seems so farfetched or ridiculous to us anymore.

"And this was no accident; it was a calculated move to make their appearance more palatable. Sci-fi is the most popular genre in films, books and comics. We were slowly indoctrinated with these concepts, until we see them as normal. I believe this is why the fallen angels have specifically bread some of their progeny to look like grey aliens or reptilians.

"Do you remember the TV program called V," Theo inquired.

"Yes, I've seen every episode," Emma acknowledged with a nod.

"The aliens came bearing gifts, the promise of blue energy. This clean energy source liberated mankind from their dependence on fossil fuel. And they brought technologically advanced medicine which brought about amazing healing. These things were interpreted as miracles by the humans. They began to worship the aliens and looked to them for the answers instead of God."

8

Kenny read a great deal about this in her uncle's notes after being released from the hospital. However, so much had happened since then that it was good to get a refresher on the topic. As she watched Elijah's niece, it was clear that she found this information awe-inspiring.

"The Vatican is preparing the world to welcome an alien Savior," Theo continued. "They'll likely tell people that they've brought a DNA upgrade which, will cause them to be immortal. I don't believe they will be immortal; however, it could cause them to live for a long time. Of course, they won't call it the mark of the beast. They will probably call it something cool like a superman download. The anti-Christ will be the genetic son of Satan; he will be a chimaera. And using the mark of the beast he will pass on this malevolent genetic strain to the world.

"It really will be a way for people to alter themselves at the genetic level. If you take this mark of the beast, it will change your DNA. You'll become Nephilim. And the Bible clearly states that there is no grace and mercy for this abomination. If you take the mark you are damned to hell. How do we know this will be the case? Jesus said that in the last days; it would be as in the days of Noah. How was it then? Fallen angels were manifesting themselves upon the earth and mingling their seed with the seed of man and beast. This is the great deception."

"But surely there will be people who make the case for Christ," Emma insisted.

"I know that many have varying opinions about when the church will be raptured from the earth. It's my opinion we will be gone before the anti-Christ is manifest upon the stage of world history. So, at this point the Christians are gone. For the most part, those who remain have rejected the truth and so they will believe the lie. Yes, there will be many saved during the tribulation. I believe these people knew the truth, but never accepted Jesus as savior.

"And if some brave soul should raise a question about Jesus being the son of God. I believe they'll be told that the writers of the Bible were simply mistaken. They'll tell them that he was actually the progeny of their alien ancestors, and that's how he could do miracles."

Emma sat quietly blinking at Theo, as if trying to take all this in. Glancing away she sighed. "I do recall hearing that the Pope called the leaders of many religions to Rome so they could pray to the same God. If the head of the church is corrupt, where does that leave the members of the Catholic faith?"

Theo smiled, "Thankfully; we answer only for our own actions. You may wish to contact your friends and ask them to watch tomorrows program. I'll do my very best to make a solid case for Christ. You should do the same. More than anything though, we must pray that the Holy Spirit takes the seeds we plant and makes them grow."

At last, Emma smiled, "Yes, let's pray right now. And then, if I can borrow a laptop for a while, I have a number of people I would like to contact."

Bowing their heads, they clasped hands as Theo led them in prayer. When he was finished, he looked to Ned.

"I've decided we should pre-record our program for tomorrow. I don't want it to be a live feed that can easily be traced."

"No problem," Ned assured, "And, I can bounce the signal off multiple servers using a proxy chain."

"Can I help," Emma asked enthusiastically.

Ned smiled, "Of course, and then you can show me how you hacked the underground feed."

Kenny smiled to herself. It seemed they had a mutual appreciation for one another's talent. Hopefully, she thought; it would take his mind off the loss of his friend.

"Here," Ned said and handed her his laptop, "You can use mine while we're filming. When you're finished, you can help us edit the program."

"Thank you," she said with true appreciation as she accepted his computer. Looking to her uncle she urged, "Let's go contact everyone we know back in the states."

"Alright," Elijah agreed and they moved to a table in the kitchen area to do their work.

"We can set up in one of the bedrooms so it will be quiet," Ned said as both he and Theo left the room.

"How is your finger?" Turner inquired once they were alone.

"It's nearly healed over. Nevertheless, Lily wants me to keep it covered and treat it with antibiotic ointment for the next week, just to be safe."

"Is it still so painful," he asked studying her carefully.

"If it wasn't bandaged, I'd have a hard time remembering it even happened. It hasn't hurt the least little bit for the last two days."

A smile quickly split his handsome face. “I’m glad to hear that...”

Lex came rushing into the room right at that moment. “Lily says she can only marry me if you give us your blessing.” His eyes were wide with concern and pleading with Turner.

“She’s a grown woman, why would she need my okay,” he said sounding baffled.

Lex sighed, “I don’t know exactly; I was nervous about asking her. I babbled on about something; I don’t even know what it was, probably something stupid. I was trying to build up my courage. Finally, I just blurted out, will you marry me.

“When her first word wasn’t either yes or no, I just stood there dazed like a deer in the headlights. I know she mentioned something about that you had gotten Theo’s blessing. She also said that you were her only living relative. So..." he spread his hands in a helpless fashion.

Turner smiled, “You would be equally yoked. You’re in love with each other. And honestly, I doubt she could find a better man to call her husband. You can tell her that I give you my blessing to marry.”

The man’s eyes fell closed with relief, “Thank you,” he whispered meaningfully. Putting his hand to his chest, he shook his head. “This is scarier than any battle I’ve ever been in.”

Kenny smiled at the notion that anything could frighten this mountain of a man.

Turner stood up and went to Lex. Patting him on the back he said, “Let’s go talk to her.”

They walked out together. Kenny moved to the kitchen to pour a cup of coffee. Smiling to herself, she pictured another wedding taking place. She was so pleased when she learned her uncle was an ordained minister. Not only was he there to share in the joy of her wedding day, he married them. It was such an unexpected, and delightful surprise.

Hopefully, it would raise the spirits of the team. It seemed everyone had been a bit down since the loss of their friend. Frowning suddenly, she wondered again about the freak lightning storm that took Cindy’s life. It was something she’d wanted to ask about, but resisted the temptation so as not to upset the others. She would wait to ask her uncle when they were alone, she determined. The problem was, with all of them traveling and living so closely together; privacy was hard to achieve.

She yawned, not having slept well the past two nights seemed to be catching up to her. Sipping her coffee, she sat down at the table where Elijah and Emma were working.

“How’s it going,” she inquired, hoping the caffeine and conversation would wake her up.

"We're doing pretty good," Elijah commented. "We composed a letter that would work for most of the people we wanted to contact. There are a few we'll write a more personal note to. Now we are sending it to the nearly fifty folks we could think of. We also encouraged them to have their friends and family watch tomorrows program as well."

"I saved the letter to Ned's laptop," Emma explained. "That way if we think of anyone we missed we could send it to them later."

"Sounds good," Kenny acknowledged with a tired smile, "Did you by chance send it to your ex-wife?"

Nodding Elijah pulled a face, "She is one of those to whom I will write a separate letter. I imagine she'll think I'm crazy. Even so, on the off chance, she does watch it; she'll know the truth. I don't want her left behind to face God's wrath."

Kenny reached across the table and patted the top of Elijah's hand in a comforting fashion. It was clear to her that he still had feelings for the woman. "You're doing all you can to help her. As a group, and individually we need to cover Carol with prayer. Time is short."

Covering her mouth, Kenny yawned again, "I'm sorry," she apologized. "It's not the company, I just haven't slept well since Cindy passed."

"Why don't you lay down and rest for a while," Elijah suggested as he rose from his seat. "I'll show you which room is yours."

"Thank you, I think I will" she acknowledged and followed after him.

Once she was alone and snuggled warm under the covers, she quickly said a prayer for Carol, and all the others they contacted. She'd barely said amen before drifting off.

Turner entered the kitchen area glancing around for Kenny. He wanted her to hear the announcement from the happy couple.

"Your wife was exhausted, so I showed her to your room." Elijah informed. "She said she hadn't slept well since the incident at Miguel's vineyard."

Pulling a face Turner nodded. "She tried not to disturb me, but I knew she wasn't resting. I think Kenny and Cindy had gotten to be good friends."

"We could hold off making our announcement until she's awake," Lily suggested.

"Yeah," Lex agreed, "That would give us a chance to slip into town and purchase our wedding rings."

Turner pursed his lips, "I'm sure she'd appreciate it. Oh, and by the way, the money I gave you for the rings, that's our wedding gift to you."

"That's a lot of money..." Lily began to protest.

Shaking his head, he held up a hand, "It's a gift, no argument."

Lily's dark-brown eyes filled with moisture, "Thank you," she whispered emotionally. Putting her arms around his neck, she hugged him tight.

"You're welcome," he said and gently patted her back. "I love you and want you to be happy, like I am."

"Shall we go," Lex asked when she released Turner.

Nodding enthusiastically, she said, "Yes, let's try to get back before Kenny wakes up."

Turner couldn't help but smile as he watched them leaving. Moments of pure joy were few and far between these days. Because of that fact, he knew it was important to cherish them when they did come along.

"I think I'm going to join Theo and Ned," he informed as he turned back to Elijah and his niece. "If you're finished, you could sit in on the taping as well."

"We still have several others to contact, but thanks for the invitation," Elijah spoke with appreciation.

Nodding in acknowledgement, Turner moved to the door where they were filming the program. He silently turned the doorknob and peered inside; Theo motioned for him to come in.

"Ned is experiencing a few problems with the camera," Theo explained as Turner sat down beside him. "It's almost as if someone is trying to prevent us from getting this information out to the world."

"Yeah," Ned agreed with a disheartened sigh, "I'm going to have to go into town and see if I can buy a new one. It was truly strange, the minute we started to film the program; a tiny puff of smoke came out of the camera. It's toast."

"I don't imagine the evil one wants anyone forewarned," Turner speculated. "We are made in the image of God; that's why he hates us."

"Yes," Theo agreed easily.

Getting to his feet, Ned stuffed the old camera into his pocket, "I'll return as soon as I can."

"Alright," Theo accepted, "do you need any money?"

"No, I'm good," he assured as he disappeared out the door.

"Where is your wife at the moment," Theo inquired studying Turner intently.

"She hasn't been sleeping well since Cindy...passed. Elijah showed her the room where we will stay, and she laid down for a nap."

"I thought she seemed tired," Theo admitted, "It'll be good for her to get some rest. Besides, I have something I'd like to speak to you about privately."

Turner's turquoise eyes studied the man for a moment. He'd known the professor long enough to know when he was about to say something he'd find troubling. "I get the feeling; I'm not going to like this."

"Well," He sighed, "I'm hoping I'm wrong, but it's something I've had on my mind for a while. I need to voice my concerns to someone I trust to tell me straight out what they think."

Giving a quick nod, Turner said, "That's the way I roll."

The professor smiled, "I know, and I appreciate that more than I can tell you."

"Okay, so what's been eating at you?"

Blinking for a moment he seemed to be gathering his thoughts. "Remember when Kenny said that a woman came to their family's house speaking of genetic enhancement?"

Turner already didn't like the way this was going, "Yeah," he answered with hesitation.

"She said the woman got really angry, and her dad had to throw her out..."

"That's right, so what is it that's worrying you," He asked with concern.

"I think they've been out to get Kenny for a very long time. And, I think it might be my fault."

9

Leaning against the dresser in their bedroom, Turner watched his lovely wife sleeping peacefully. He couldn't get the conversation with her uncle out of his head. If she had any idea of his concerns, she would not be able to rest so serenely. He thought with a shake of his head.

"Why do you think it's your fault," Turner had queried.

"Ten years ago, when we started out on this journey, Kenny was twelve years old. She was already an Olympian class swimmer at that point. You know the old saying; know your enemy?"

"Yes, of course," Turner assured him.

"I became an enemy to the dark side the instant; I began placing these videos online. When I was in the FEMA camp, I saw plainly how they used the threat of harm to loved ones to attempt to coerce their compliance. I know they looked into my family history to find my Achilles heel.

"I don't believe they intended to kill Kenny when the rest of her family was murdered. She was out of town, tending to her sick aunt, remember?"

"You think they didn't realize she'd just returned," Turner quizzed.

"That's what I believe. I think the slaughter of my sister's family was two-fold in its intent. They wanted to control me, and they wanted to capture Kenny. I'm afraid one of those vile creatures has a fascination for her due to her superior physique and abilities.

"You know their plan was to capture her the night we brought her into the fold. On the island, they activated some of their cloaked Nephilim in an attempt to imprison her. And what did they do the moment; they actually got their hands on her; they cloned an army of super soldiers from her DNA. That's not even mentioning the technologically advanced RFID tag they placed on her finger so they could track her if she got away from them."

Turner could easily remember the sick feeling in his gut at that point. "What are you trying to say, Theo? Do you think her family was killed in part because they wanted her?"

The man's head bobbed forward, "I didn't at first, I accepted full responsibility for what happened. But now I'm not so sure. I asked Ned to carefully preserve her fingertip and send it to a doctor who has removed implants for us before.

I'm not sure why I did it, but I did. I asked them to test to see what kind of poison they'd used."

"And" Turner encouraged, almost hating to ask, nevertheless, needing to know the answer.

"It wasn't poison, Turner; it was triple helix DNA..." Theo revealed, his voice shaky. "They'd mixed her blood with Nephilim. As you know, we've spoken many times about their desire to turn men into monsters. Now before you get too excited, I also sent them the towels that were used to wrap her wound. What's equally important is that I sent them the bandages Lily changed every day. That blood, was Kenny's alone. So, rest assured she was not infected with their DNA."

"They were planning on turning her into a hybrid," Turner whispered, horrified with the thought. "Don't get me wrong, but if that was the plan, why didn't they just do it when they held her captive?"

"I'm not altogether sure," Theo confessed. "It could be that they wanted to clone her physical attributes first. Perhaps, they couldn't because she was pregnant. Alternatively, and this seems more likely; they were waiting for a specified time, the appearance of the anti-Christ."

Theo leaned across the table and spoke softly, "It wouldn't have worked, Turner. She's a child of God. Kenny did not take their mark willingly, nor did she deny God. Even so, it shows their determination as far as she's concerned."

Going to the side of their bed, he knelt down beside his wife. Closing his eyes, he prayed fervently for her protection. When he opened his eyes, he was struck again by how beautiful she was. It was true that a woman just seemed to glow when carrying a child, he thought and smiled. The smile quickly slid from his face, however, as he realized an overwhelming need to protect her and the baby.

"Help me, Lord," he whispered barely audible. "Strengthen me and give me wisdom for the coming days, in Jesus name I pray."

Leaning forward he gently kissed her cheek. As he did he heard Lily and Lex returning from their errand. Kenny's eyelids slowly fluttered open. Upon seeing him she smiled.

"Hi," she whispered sweetly.

"Hi," he responded in kind, "Lily and Lex are going to make an announcement. I thought you would like to hear it," he said as he got to his feet.

Her expression warmed, "Yes, I would."

"Did you get enough rest," he asked as she got out of bed and retrieved her wedding ring from the night stand.

"I feel much better; I think I really conked out."

"I love you," Turner said meaningfully and kissed her forehead.

"I love you, too," she said and wrapped her arms around his waist. She briefly rested her head against his chest before saying, "I'd better brush my hair, so we can go and hear their announcement."

When she was ready, they went out to join the others who had gathered around the couple.

"Good, you're awake," Lily said sounding relieved, "Do you want to tell them," she said looking to Lex.

"I've asked this beautiful woman to marry me, and she has agreed."

The whole group took turns hugging and congratulating them.

"Were you able to find a jewelry store," Turner inquired then.

"Well, no," Lily said, "but we were able to buy our wedding rings."

"How did you do that," Turner quizzed.

"You know my Spanish is not the best, right?"

"Yeah," He agreed easily.

"Well, I thought I asked for directions to a jewelry store. However, we ended up on a street with a lot of cute little houses. It was then that I noticed an elderly woman sitting on her front steps. Her elbows were on her knees, and her face rested in her hands. She looked so sad that I almost didn't bother her.

"But you know how you sometimes feel a nudging from the Holy Spirit? So, I tried to ask her in Spanish where we could find wedding rings. I didn't think she understood me because for a few moments she just looked at me as if in shock.

"Suddenly, she leapt to her feet and said in perfect English, 'wait here.' She disappeared into the house for only a few seconds. When she returned, she carried this little box." Lily explained and pulled a flat black box approximately three inches' square from her pocket.

Taking off the lid, his sister carefully unfolded the napkin they were wrapped in. There lay a man's gold band and a stunning diamond ring.

"Oh, my gosh," Kenny said with awe, "They are beautiful, but do they fit?"

"They fit perfectly," Lex answered sounding amazed. "She told us that she had prayed all night for the Lord to help her financially. Her husband passed two months ago, with one payment left owing on their house. If she couldn't make the payment by the end of the week, she would be thrown out on the street. She said she would sell us the rings for the $500-dollar payment she needed.

"As you can plainly see, they are worth much more than that. The bands are 14 carat gold and the three diamonds would likely be worth more than that all by themselves. So, I gave her the entire $800 that you'd given us as a wedding gift."

"She started to cry and began praising God," Lily said as a line of moisture rose up in her dark-brown eyes. "She said she would tell everyone how God had answered her desperate prayers."

Turner smiled and gave his sister a hug, "Sounds like it was a God ordained meeting."

"When will the ceremony take place," Kenny said sounding excited.

"Right now, if you've finished taping your program," Lily said looking to Theo.

"Well..." Theo began but stopped when he saw Ned entering the room.

"I got another camera," Ned announced holding up a package. "What's going on," he asked when he saw everyone gathered around the happy couple.

"Lex and Lily are going to be married," Theo said then. "The taping will have to wait for a bit."

"Congratulations," Ned said as he came and shook both Lex and Lily's hands.

"Oh, come on, you can do better than that," Lily encouraged as she hugged him.

"Yeah but I didn't want Lex to smack me for getting fresh," he informed as he smiled at the big guy.

"No worries," Lex assured, "this is the happiest day of my life."

"Everyone is here, should we begin," Theo inquired bearing a huge grin.

Turner noted that it obviously gave Theo a great deal of joy to be able to join two lives together.

"Dearly beloved," Theo began as he stood before the group. "We are gathered here today for the purpose of joining Lex and Lily together in holy matrimony..."

Turner stood with his arm around Kenny on one side, Ned, Emma and Elijah grouped together on the other side.

"Lex, will you have this woman to be your wife?"

"I will," he assured with a nod of his head.

Looking to Turner's sister Theo asked, "Will you have this man to be your husband?"

"I will," she answered her voice high with emotion.

"Does anyone here object to these proceedings?"

"Hey, you didn't ask that question at Turner's wedding," Lex protested before laughing heartily.

Everyone had a good laugh, “I know,” Theo admitted. “But I’ve always wanted to ask that question. And, who knows this might be my last opportunity.”

“There are no objections to this marriage,” Turner offered then. “In fact, you are a welcome addition to this family.”

“Before you exchange rings I’d like to say a few words. Keep your devotion to God first and foremost. Cherish one another always. Never miss an opportunity to show love. Remember, communication is the life blood of any relationship. Due to the lateness of the hour, you may not have an occasion where you need to forgive. But should you find yourself in that position, forgive quickly. Something else I’ve learned through the years, is that fear often manifests itself as anger. If you ever find yourself feeling angry with your spouse, ask yourself what you’re afraid of.”

10

"Lily and Lex will return from their short three-day honeymoon in a little while," Kenny heard her uncle saying to Turner.

"When they get back, we'll go and secure the cache of weapons you arranged for yesterday," her husband said in response.

Everyone was doing their part to get ready to set sail, all but Kenny that is. They were still treating her with kid gloves and not allowing her to do much. Feeling bored and not certain, how long they'd be cooped up on the yacht, Kenny decided she would go for a swim for exercise.

Not wanting to disturb their strategy meeting she wrote her husband a note and left it on the table in the kitchen.

Slicing silently into the water, she hoped their child would love to swim as much as she did. Thinking about it, she realized that she'd never asked Turner how he felt about the water. She knew it would take time for them to get to know each other completely. And, she conceded; their first year of marriage would not be typical.

Forever being on the move, and facing danger nearly at every turn, might cause a delay in full disclosure.

She wondered about where they were headed next. Theo held true to his habit of sharing destination information with a select few. She was reminded of what Emma said about there being no real safe place in the world anymore. So, she told herself, it really didn't matter where they were headed.

Right here and now she was thoroughly enjoying the cool clear waters of the South Pacific Ocean, and that's what she chose to focus on. After frolicking in the water for about forty minutes, she returned to the area where Elijah's boat was anchored. Climbing onto the dock she felt refreshed and invigorated.

"Where have you been," Turner shouted angrily from the deck of the yacht.

Frowning she walked to the short ladder and climbed onto the boat. "I told you…" she began to explain.

"You did not," he insisted hotly. "I was having a meeting with Theo and when I came to tell you our plans you were nowhere to be found."

Kenny found herself taken aback by the ferocity of his tone. Walking into the cabin her intent was to show him the note he'd obviously overlooked. As she went, she averted her glance in order to avoid eye contact with the rest of the crew. She felt mortified by the way he'd spoken to her in front of them.

However, the note wasn't where she'd left it. Looking around the kitchen area she couldn't spot it.

"I left a note right here on the table telling you where I was going," she informed as she looked on the floor.

"Did anybody see a note," Turner demanded of the rest of the group.

Kenny watched in disbelief as each member denied having seen it. The very fact that her husband asked the others meant that he didn't believe her. Hurt and angry she started toward their bedroom.

Grabbing her painfully at the elbow Turner spoke through clenched teeth. "From here on out you are not to go anywhere alone, do you understand?"

"You're hurting me," she cried and jerked her arm free. Going to their room she shut and locked the door behind her.

Turner immediately knocked on the door, "I need to talk to you," he said in a conciliatory tone.

"Go away," she answered quietly, "This liar is done talking to you."

Tears streamed down her face as she made her way to the shower. She hoped the water would drown out anything further he might have to say. Feeling dejected, she sighed, twenty minutes ago; she'd felt so alive and wonderful during her swim. And now, she felt emotionally as if she were stranded at the bottom of a well. Amazing how quickly your outlook could take such a drastic turn, she mused.

She couldn't understand what happened to the note she'd left for him. Surely someone must have seen it; she reasoned. Regardless, he had no right to speak to her that way she thought with resentment.

And then, as if the Holy Spirit brought it to mind, she recalled her uncle's words at the wedding. Fear often manifests itself as anger. Frowning she wondered why he would have been so fearful for her safety today. Perhaps, since the incident in Panama City, he's felt that way on a regular basis, she considered.

Kenny suddenly felt the need to speak to Turner as soon as possible. Satan was the one who came to steal, kill and destroy. She wasn't about to let him ruin her marriage. Drying off she dressed herself hurriedly. Beginning two weeks ago, she'd had to start wearing maternity clothes. Everything she owned had become uncomfortably tight.

"Where is Turner," she inquired of her uncle when she found him sitting at the kitchen table alone.

"Lex, Lily, Turner and Ned went to pick up the ammo I bought from a man in town. Elijah and Emma went to the grocery store for supplies." He answered soberly.

Pulling in a deep breath, she released it slowly. "Could we walk up and down the dock for exercise while we talk?"

Theo got up from the table and came to stand beside her, "Sure honey, are you alright?"

"I'm fine," she answered shaking her head in a dismissive fashion as they made their way out to the dock. "However, I'm a bit confused about what happened. All I wanted to do was to get some exercise before we set sail. I left a note; I swear I did."

Locking arms with her as they walked side by side he assured, "I believe you, sweetie. I know that Turner does as well."

"It didn't sound as if he believed me," she quipped, feeling slightly irritated once more.

"That man loves you more than his own life, Kenny. I know him and there isn't anything he wouldn't do to keep you safe. When he came out of our meeting and couldn't find you, I think he assumed the worst. He began frantically searching everywhere for you. By the time, you showed up he was about half out of his mind with worry. That's what you witnessed, his emotional meltdown when he thought he'd lost you."

Hot tears filled her eyes as she stopped walking and leaned against a post at the end of the dock. "Making him crazy is the last thing I want to do, Theo. I love him with my whole heart. I couldn't have asked for a better husband." She assured as she threw her hands up in a helpless manner. "My God, all I wanted was a little exercise."

"Sweetheart," Theo said and pulled a half smile, "It's not the end of the world. Every married couple has misunderstandings and arguments; you'll get past it; I promise."

Pulling a face, she gave a curt nod, and wiped her face. "I'd like to ask you about something else while no one is around."

"What is it," Theo inquired.

"How is it that lightning came out of a cloudless sky the day that Cindy died?"

"Well," Theo sighed, "there are a couple of possible explanations. Have you ever heard the expression 'a bolt out of the blue'?"

Kenny shook her head, "No I've never heard that before."

"Lightning can travel up to twenty-five miles from the storm that generated it. So, there could have been a squall behind the mountains that we couldn't see."

Studying her uncle's face, she asked, "Do you believe that's what happened?"

He gave a quick shake of his head, "No I don't. I watched the news that day and there was no mention of a storm anywhere in the area."

Frowning, she felt confused, "How could it happen then?"

"Do you remember Matthew 24:29, Immediately after the tribulation of those days shall the sun be darkened, and the moon shall not give her light, and the stars shall fall from heaven, and the powers of the heavens shall be shaken. And, Luke 21:26, Men's hearts failing them for fear, and for looking after those things which are coming on the earth: for the powers of heaven shall be shaken?"

"I remember," Kenny assured him.

"In both those verses, it speaks of the powers of heaven being shaken, and stars falling from heaven. If you've been listening to others on social media who are trying to get the word out, you've undoubtedly heard of Nibiru or planet X. Actually, they seem to call it by many names. I think that's just to confuse people."

"I've heard of it," she admitted, "but I honestly didn't know if that was fact or fiction.

With everything else that's happened; I haven't had an opportunity to look into it."

Blinking thoughtfully, her uncle adjusted his glasses. "Understand that I am not an expert in this area. I'll attempt to explain it to the best of my ability. However, clearly we'll both need to do some more research."

"Alright," she acknowledged, "for now; I'm just looking for a basic understanding of what took Cindy's life."

"There are those who believe we live in a binary system, and that Nibiru is part of that system. They say that it is causing atmospheric compression on the earth which fills the air with chargeable particles that can manifest as thunder bolts. There is also the theory that the chargeable particles are due to a brown dwarf exploding, and the waves of energy from that blast are just now beginning to reach us. I'm not sure which theory is true. Nevertheless, I know the word of God warned us that the powers of heaven shall be shaken."

Burning tears filled her eyes and quickly spilled down her cheeks. She wasn't sure why she was crying, other than she missed Cindy terribly.

"Oh, honey," Theo comforted and pulled her into his arms. "I know the two of you had become close, but I promise you she's in a much better place."

"I know," Kenny whispered, "I know."

11

Turner sat in the back of the van they'd rented to pick up the ammo, scrunched down in the seat, his elbow on the arm rest, his hand covering his eyes. He couldn't believe the way he'd acted with his wife earlier. Would she ever forgive him? He wondered? He was reminded of Theo begging him not to hurt her; and yet he had.

Sighing audibly, he felt like the scum of the earth.

"Turner," Lily said cautiously, "you haven't said a word since we left the ship. She loves you, just explain how worried you were; she'll understand."

"How can I make her understand when I can't comprehend my own behavior?"

"Honey…" Lily began.

"Please, Lily…" he sighed, "I just have to pray she'll believe that I never meant to hurt her."

"We all know that," Ned said quietly, "I'm guessing Theo had a talk with you. He told you what we learned when we sent the RFID they tagged her with to the lab, didn't he?"

"Yes," Turner acknowledged and straightened up in his seat.

"What did they learn," Lily questioned suspiciously just as Lex pulled into the parking lot near Elijah's yacht.

"What is that," Lex demanded as he pointed to just past where Theo and Kenny were standing.

Grabbing his rifle, Turner leapt from the vehicle. Suddenly all of the passengers were standing at the front of the van.

"I've never seen one before, but I think it's an interdimensional portal opening up. You need to tell them to get out of there before something comes through," Ned advised, shouting nervously.

It was just at that moment his wife, and the leader of their group took notice of the anomaly. The spatial distortion gave the impression of liquid silver looping back on itself. It was both frightening and mesmerizing at the same time. Kenny pulled the Glock from under her left arm as they swiftly backed away.

"Get out of there," the others shouted frantically in unison as Turner took aim with the dragon.

And then, what looked like a wave of water rotating in a tight circle came blasting out of it. When it hit Theo, it sent him sailing through the air backwards down the dock about twenty feet.

"Theo," Kenny screamed back over her shoulder, "are you alright?"

Keeping her target in view she moved to where her uncle appeared to lie unconscious on the dock. Immediately several of the reptilians emerged. Accurately firing her Glock, Kenny took out ten of them while retrieving her pistol from her right holster.

The other members of the team quickly gathered their guns from the van. Turner knew she had seven more bullets in the Glock and fifteen rounds in the Walther P99. They began advancing rapidly toward the wharf, weapons drawn.

He could hear his wife entreating her uncle to respond, however, she wasn't getting an answer. Glancing briefly to where he lay, he could see blood near his mouth and on his forehead. Even so, he didn't have time to pray before more of those critters came blasting through to this side.

"My God, what's happening," Turner heard Elijah exclaim, and Emma gasp from behind them.

"Stay back," he hollered over his shoulder.

Keeping a mental count, Turner knew his wife would soon be out of ammo. "They don't appear to have any weapons," he shouted to the others. "Ned, Lily, I want you to run over and give your pistols to Kenny. And then, drag Theo out of harm's way. We'll keep you covered."

Wasting no time, they ran down to the dock to carry out his orders. They had just managed to gently pull Theo to the boat ladder when the next entity emerged. Everyone's mouth dropped open when they witnessed the sentient robot from Emma's video step into this dimension.

He stood about nine or ten feet tall, and was built like one of those powerful wrestlers. "My God," Turner whispered, "help us, Lord."

"Can this thing handle salt water," Kenny yelled back to Ned.

Ned was shaking his head, "I don't know…I doubt it, but I can't say for sure."

Kicking off her shoes, Kenny tossed Ned and Lily their weapons before slicing into the water. She swam out several yards and looked back to see what he would do. As she must have suspected the thing dove in after her. The rift immediately closed and disappeared.

"Get the boat loaded I'll be back in a bit," She yelled and turned, taking off like the Olympian that she was.

"Hurry we have to get the ammo," Turner yelled to Lex. It felt like it took forever to get Theo and the supplies onboard. In reality, it took only ten minutes. Grabbing their binoculars, the men rushed to the upper deck to see if they could spot

Kenny or the robot. The women stayed with Theo to tend to his injuries. For three long minutes, they couldn't find her.

"Come on, Kenny, come on, show us where you are, sweetheart," Turner urged as he searched the area.

"I don't see any sign of either one of them," Ned shouted.

"Start the engine," Turner yelled to Elijah as he reached into the front pocket of his Jean jacket. Pulling out five bullets, he quickly loaded them into the dragon.

"Those are the armor-piercing rounds you've been saving," Lex observed.

"Yes," Turner acknowledged swallowing hard, "let's pray they will work on that thing."

"I see them," Ned yelled excitedly just as the yacht's engine rumbled to life.

"Show me," Turner insisted as he moved closer to Ned's position.

Lifting his binoculars, he could see the sun glinting off the monster. "I see the robot, but where is my wife?"

"She's about thirty yards in front of him," Lex informed him sounding relieved at having spotted her.

"Yes, I see her now, thank God," Turner said sounding comforted. "Elijah, she's straight out about a quarter mile."

Pulling the boat out of the slip, Elijah sped up rapidly. As he neared her location, he slowed up and pointed the ship toward the north. That way, the ladder was where Kenny could climb on easily.

Running toward the back of the boat, Turner yelled, "Help her on board. I'm going to keep this thing in my sights. Ned, what should I aim for?"

"Try for the eye socket first," Ned shouted back. "If that doesn't work, aim for the lower right-hand quadrant of the torso."

"Hurry, and get her out of the water," Turner yelled excitedly, "That thing is picking up speed."

Kenny appeared exhausted when Lex pulled her up onto the ladder. "Go inside, I'm going to be Turner's wing man," he assured her.

"Step on it," Turner hollered to Elijah just as the robot caught hold of the metal railing at the bottom of the ladder.

"Take her inside the cabin," he shouted frantically while taking aim. The bullet went straight through the eye socket and out the other side. Nevertheless, the monster kept coming.

"Dear God, I need you, please help me," Turner prayed as he watched the robot climbing the stairs. When he'd come out of the water enough that Turner could get a shot at the lower right-hand section of its torso, he fired again.

Sparks flew in all directions as the thing jerked violently, “You will die,” he growled angrily.

“Yeah well, we’re all going to die at some point,” Turner responded in a focused monotone.

It was clear by his actions that the last shot had done some major damage. However, Turner was impatient for the thing to be gone. Pulling the trigger once more, the round tore through the robot’s chest cavity causing him to lose his grip on the railing. His heavy-metal frame bounced off the top of the water once and then promptly began to sink.

Relief washed over him in waves. “Thank you, Jesus,” he whispered several times before rushing into the cabin to find his wife.

She was standing in the middle of the room, dripping wet, watching him. Her expression said that she didn’t know what to expect from him. Tears burned at the back of his eyes as he went to her and gently pulled her into his arms.

“Forgive me,” he pleaded; his voice choked with emotion, “I never meant to hurt you.”

“I know,” she whispered softly before pressing her lips to his. For several seconds, it was as if the world and all its problems disappeared.

“Now that goes a long way toward making this old man feel better,” Theo acknowledged.

Pulling away, Kenny went to kneel down in front of her uncle. “Thank God you’re alive,” she said with high emotion, “I was afraid they had killed you.”

“Is he going to be alright,” Turner inquired of his sister.

“We’ll need to watch for signs of a concussion because it appears, he did hit his head pretty hard,” Lily explained as her concerned glance poured over Theo several times. “I found no broken bones. I’m sure he’s going to be very sore for several days. But it didn’t really seem as if they were trying to kill him. I think they were just trying to separate him from Kenny.”

“You’re all wet,” Theo observed with a confused frown when his glance found his niece once more.

“Yeah,” she responded through a half laugh. “I wanted to get some exercise today, and I must say I certainly got it.”

“You missed all the excitement. You were knocked unconscious by that water cannon just before a horde of reptilians came through the portal,” Ned informed.

“When the first wave of attack couldn’t get, the job done, they sent in the robot we observed on Emma’s video,” Lex explained further.

Theo's eyes grew large, "My God," He whispered seemingly horrified, "They must be getting desperate."

"About what," Kenny questioned. "Yes, you're putting out videos bringing their works to light. Even so, you're hardly the only one. While I've been recuperating, I've spent a lot of time listening to others who are doing the same thing online."

"While you're answering questions," Ned broke in, "how did they find us again?"

Holding his mid-section Theo gingerly scooted out to the edge of the couch where he was resting. Pulling in a deep breath he adjusted his wire rimmed glasses.

"Many years ago, while doing some research, I came across an obscure paper. At the time, I thought it was ridiculous. It was talking about Joseph Jacob's 1890 rendition of Jack and the Beanstalk. You undoubtedly remember the giant saying; Fee-Fi-Fo-Fum I smell the blood of an Englishman. Be he alive or be he dead, I'll grind his bones to make my bread. I didn't even finish reading it.

"Years later when I discovered the giants were cannibals; I found that paper again and read every last word. Cultures all over the world had stories like these that they handed down to each generation. The native American Indians had oral traditions telling of gods that came through portals. The whole reason they began the practice of holding up their hands in greeting, is to see how many fingers the stranger had. The giants had six fingers and toes, Goliath of Gath, the giant whom David slew had six fingers and toes. So, the Bible backs this up.

"Many of these children's stories, such as Grimm's fairy tales, were written by an author under demonic influence. Demons are the disembodied spirits of the giants. Fairies, gnomes, Trolls, Elves and the like were real creatures, the product of genetic engineering by the watchers. When you think about it, most of the fairy tales possess a macabre undertone. Take jack and the beanstalk, for example; the giant openly admits he intends to eat his target. How will he know his target, by the smell of his blood?

"And, as you know, they have samples of Kenny's blood. That's how they were able in part to make their super soldier army..."

"My God," Kenny whispered, disturbed by the implication of her uncle's words.

Reaching out, Theo took hold of her hands. "A few days ago, I had a conversation with your husband about my concerns. I'm pretty sure that's the reason why he overreacted when he couldn't find you this morning. I didn't really want to share my thoughts on the matter with you, even so, I don't see as I have a choice."

"Do I want to hear this," She asked with a note of hesitation.

Theo's eyes closed and he drew a deep breath, "Sweetheart, do you recall telling us that a woman approached your parents about genetic enhancement?"

"Yeah," she answered suspiciously.

"Let me back fill with information for a moment. While I was held prisoner in the FEMA camp, our captors let it be known that they knew everything about our families. The moment I began to shine a spotlight on their activities and agenda; they made sure to find my Achilles heel. For me, that is you," he explained and pulled a sad smile.

"But you loved my momma every bit as much," Kenny insisted gently.

"I loved Diana deeply, you know that. She knew that I could never have a child of my own. To try to make up for that she chose me as your godfather and allowed me to participate in every aspect of your life. At times, it felt as if you were my child, we had so much fun together. Do you remember?"

"I do," she assured with a smile.

Shaking his head in a thoughtful manner, "You have no way of knowing how special that was for me. I thought I would never experience the close bond that a parent has with their child. However, I had that with you," he said and kissed her hands.

"What is it that you're afraid of, Theo," she questioned softly.

"I've come to believe that one of those evil entities straight out of the pit of hell has set his mind on having you," he blurted out. "That tag they put on your little finger didn't carry a lethal dose as we feared. It was triple helix DNA. Your blood mixed with that of a Nephilim. At a set time, they intended to release it into your bloodstream and turn you into a monster. They apparently didn't know you were saved by the blood of Christ, and so their plan would never have worked.

"Ten years ago, when I started doing these YouTube videos, you were twelve years old. At that young age, you were already handily beating all competitors at your swimming matches. I reason that when they went looking for my weakness, one of them found a weakness of their own. I think when they approached your parents with the prospect of genetic enhancement, the plan was to do much more than just heighten your abilities. You told us that when your dad said no she became angry, right?"

Kenny's glance wandered as she brought back the memory of that day. "Her face turned red and she was absolutely livid. She began screaming that it would be done whether we liked it or not. That's when my dad physically threw her out of our house."

"Were you ever approached by anyone else with this idea," Turner inquired then.

Shaking her head, she answered quietly, trepidation sounding in her voice, "No."

"Perhaps they simply decided to wait until a designated time. A time closer to when the evil one was to make his appearance," Theo said thoughtfully.

"I feel like there is something more you're not telling me," Kenny said as her light-brown eyes searched first her uncles face and then his.

Resigned, Turner pulled in a stabilizing breath and let it go. "We think it's possible they intended to take you after they killed your family. You had been tending to your aunt, and it's conceivable they didn't realize you had returned."

His wife's face seemed to lose all color, as her light-brown eyes held his glance. At first, she seemed stunned. Pushing away from Theo, she got onto her feet.

"You're saying…they killed my…family, my friend because of me." She demanded in disbelief.

"Kenny," Turner attempted to calm her by going to her side and trying to take her into is arms.

"No, don't do that," she insisted as she moved away from him seemingly horrified at the thought. "Is that what you're saying?"

"Sweetheart, we don't know for sure," Theo said sounding pained as he got to his feet.

"My God," she whispered hoarsely as tears instantly filled her eyes and then streaked down her cheeks. "Oh God, no, please no," she mumbled as she made her way swiftly toward their bedroom and locked the door behind her.

12

Kenny cried until she had no tears left. It felt as if a heavy blanket was placed upon her, weighing her down until she couldn't even bring herself to speak. Several times throughout the rest of that day, members of the team would knock at her door. They would say encouraging words, trying to entice her to come out and talk with them. She never answered, unable even to summon the strength to respond.

She'd never really stopped to analyze the specific reason her family was targeted. How stupid was that? She thought with self-loathing. After reading her uncle's notes, she'd assumed it was because of the work he was doing. However, she conceded silently; her father had made an enemy when he threw that woman out of their home. And, the thought that one of those vile creatures had developed a thing for her, was both repulsive and frightening.

"Father in heaven," she whispered into the darkness of the night, "Help me, Lord."

She must have fallen asleep at some point because she realized she was dreaming, before her eyes appeared a snow-covered tundra. When she turned, and looked toward the water, she saw huge chunks of ice topped with penguins. They were flapping one arm almost as if they were waving at her.

A slow smile spread across her face, it was a beautiful and peaceful setting. And then, the dorsal fins of two killer whales broke the surface of the water. Having grown up in Seattle near Puget Sound she was very familiar with orcas. They were the largest member of the dolphin family. They were considered apex predators, because they were hunted by no other species.

She couldn't help but wonder why that information had come to mind. And what was the purpose of remembering it now?

As she continued to watch the whales, she found their behavior uncharacteristic for their kind. Clearly, they were afraid of something that was chasing them. They darted this way and that, even leaping over large chunks of ice floating in the frigid waters.

A long tentacle reached out from the deep coiling itself around one of the frightened mammals. Writhing frantically, it tried to free itself.

Many years ago, Kenny was privileged to see an illustration from the original 1870 edition of Twenty Thousand Leagues Under the Sea by author Jules Verne. The Kraken was a legendary sea monster of giant size. It resembled a squid, and it was said that just one of these creatures could take down an entire ship, or swallow a whale whole. In the Norwegian language, the word Kraken meant something twisted.

She recalled Theo speaking about the triple helix DNA of the Nephilim. Were the seafaring Vikings referring to the genetic interference of the fallen ones? She questioned silently.

Suddenly, this giant creature, which she'd always considered the figment of Jules Verne's imagination, bursts up out of the water. Alarmed, Kenny fell backward onto the snow. Scrambling to her feet, she worked to put some distance between her and the edge of the water. Glancing back over her shoulder as she worked to get away, she witnessed the Kraken swallowing the killer whale.

"Oh, my God," she whispered fearfully. Her progress was slow due to the layer of ice covering the snow. Kenny found it nearly impossible to stay on her feet because of how slippery it was. Approximately thirty feet in front of her, there was a place where the snow had receded. It was covered with rocks. If I can just get there, she thought desperately, I would be alright. Getting down on her hands and knees she grabbed whatever she could in order to slide to safety.

Just as she neared the rocky area, one of the long tentacles of the Kraken wrapped around her left calf. Releasing a frightened scream, she clung to the edge of the ice as she struggled to free herself.

The ground began to shake with the weight of something very large traveling swiftly in their direction. Each foot fall felt like a mini earthquake. Whatever was approaching seem to have distracted the Kraken, because he stopped yanking on her leg. Reaching in under her left arm, she grabbed the Glock. Still holding the ice with her left hand, she rolled over onto her back and fired, separating the piece around her leg from the rest of the tentacle. Blood flew, and the creature squealed in agony as it quickly retreated back into the water.

Kenny immediately scrambled toward an ice overhang to hide from what was approaching. Removing the last of the sea monster's appendage from her leg, she tossed it into the water.

She became aware that the ground stopped shaking. Now, however, she could hear the rapid breaths of something huge, very near her location. And then came the deafening roar of what sounded like a T-Rex. Covering her ears, she squeezed her eyes shut.

Within the nightmare, she recalled the strange sounds they'd heard at Miguel's vineyard. *Oh God,* she prayed silently, *why am I having this dream?*

Before an answer could come she heard a booming voice saying, "Fee-Fi-Fo-Fum..."

Her eyes popped open, as she sat frozen in fear waiting for him to finish his rhyme.

"The one I've chosen has finally come," he continued before erupting in fiendish laughter.

A wave of goose bumps washed down over her arms, and she shivered. Was this a dream, she wondered? Or had they found a way to take her from her room on the ship? With their advanced technology, she believed they could do it if they took a notion.

"Is this a dream, Lord," she whispered ever so quietly. Closing her eyes once more she waited for an answer. Nevertheless, the only sound she heard was the heavy breathing of the beast that brought the Nephilim to her location.

"You will have to come to me, or risk freezing to death. I rather think I'd like to see you come crawling on your hands and knees, begging for me to take you in. It might teach you some respect." He said with irritation.

She could tell by the sounds that came next, that he was climbing back up on his steed. The ground shook again as the animal turned and began to move away from her position.

Ever so carefully she inched forward until she could peek over the ice shelf. Her expression dropped when she saw the red-haired giant riding atop a Titanosaur. When she was in school, her class took a field trip to the American Museum of Natural History. They had just opened the Titanosaur exhibit. She could easily remember being amazed by the sheer size of this dinosaur. Its length on average was that of three double-Decker buses in line, or approximately one hundred and thirty feet from head to tail. And could easily reach the top of a five-story building.

Swallowing hard she realized then that the giant must be nearly fifteen feet tall. He turned to look back in her direction, and she quickly ducked back under the shelf.

However, she was curious about how a dinosaur could survive in such frigid temperatures. After waiting for a few moments, she carefully glanced over the ice shelf. Kenny noted that she could follow along behind them on the bare rocky ground for quite a distance. If the giant should turn back to look for her, she could duck below the ice.

Since she didn't know how she'd arrived at this place, she thought that the answer for escape might be found wherever they were headed. Checking her weapons, she found them fully loaded minus the one round she'd used on the Kraken. Returning her guns to their holsters she took out after them.

According to her watch, they had been on the move for a little more than an hour when the Giant leapt from the back of the Titanosaur. The animal let out an ear-piercing roar as he came to a stop. The Nephilim planted his fists on his hips as he surveilled the area.

He didn't appear to be searching for her at the moment. Kenny surmised as she watched from behind an out cropping of ice. Numerous times during the past hour she'd had to quickly hide herself when he did turn and look for her.

Frowning, Kenny wondered if he could smell her blood. Did he know exactly where she was at all times? Was she fooling herself by thinking that as long as she kept out of sight, he didn't know where she was?

"Come to me and I will take you to a place where you will be warm and worshiped. Join with me and I will give you powers above that of mere mortal men. I will share with you the forbidden knowledge of heaven."

The giant hadn't shouted, rather he'd spoken as if assured that she would hear him. In that moment, it was obvious he knew she was close by.

Hearing a sound that resembled compression brakes, she watched as a huge section of ground began to raise up in front of the giant's location. When it finally stopped, it was approximately as tall as a five-story building.

Squinting she realized that the people on the platform were high-ranking leaders of nations from all over the world. The former president of the US was among them, and they were all looking through telescopes toward the heavens. Glancing upward, she wondered what they were looking for that was so important.

It slowly grew dark as an eclipse of the sun began. Low level lighting came on around the stargazing gathering of government officials. Looking to the sky once more, she saw the ring of fire. Just to the left of it was an odd light. She wondered what it could be.

The voices from the platform rose with excitement. "I see it," one of them shouted. "It's Nibiru," another one chimed in.

Nibiru, Kenny thought with consternation. Her uncle said that planet could be the reason for the destructive waves of energy coming upon the Earth. The reason...Cindy's life ended so tragically.

As the eclipse began to wane, it appeared the elite began to dispute the matter amongst themselves. And then, she heard a noise that sounded like a hover craft. Searching the sky, she saw an armada of strange flying machines coming in their direction.

Her father was a big fan of Star Trek, and some of these craft resembled the Klingon battle cruiser from that program. And, some of them looked a lot like the ships she'd seen on Star Wars. The one that whizzed directly over her location, looked almost exactly like Darth Vader's TIE fighter.

Kenny ducked under a nearby ice shelf, not wanting to be seen. Carefully leaning forward so she could get a glimpse of the sky, she watched until they passed her position. She was reminded of what her uncle said about these advanced concepts being presented to them as fantasy through science fiction, when, in fact, they were real. *We are being conditioned to be accepting of this new reality,* Theo explained. *And, the closer we get to the unveiling of the anti-Christ the bolder they become.*

When she was certain all the ships had passed her location, she cautiously peered out. One of them landed near the platform. The others hovered silently overhead. To her complete amazement, troops donning the same garb the Nazis wore in WW2 piled out of the craft on the ground.

"I'm tired of waiting for her to come to me," the giant bellowed angrily, "find her and bring her here."

With weapons drawn, the soldiers immediately began to comb the area looking for her. Breaking off a piece of the ice, Kenny scooted as far back in the ice cave as possible, holding the chuck of ice in front to conceal herself.

"I want to wake up now," she whispered repeatedly as hot tears burned at the back of her eyes. "God please, let me wake up. He can't force me to be a part of their evil scheme. I am a child of God, saved by the blood of Jesus. You are an ever-present help in times of trouble. Help me, Lord, I need to get back to my husband and my friends."

She became aware that she was hearing a loud banging sound. Frowning she forced her eyes open. When she realized, she was safe in her bedroom on Elijah's yacht, she released a grateful sigh of relief.

"Thank you, Lord," she whispered appreciatively, "forgive me for indulging in self-pity. Whatever the reason for the deaths of my family, I know they are with you, and I will see them again. I love you, Jesus..."

Her prayer was cut short when Lily banged loudly on her door, “Kenny, wake up we have to prepare to face a major tsunami. There has been a full rupture of the Cascadia Subduction zone. It was a 9.0; the entire ring of fire is alive with activity.”

13

Her mouth dropped open as she leapt from the bed and went to open the door. She locked glances with her sister-in-law. "It was a full rupture of the interplate," Lily explained with tears in her eyes. "They are predicting a tsunami worse than the one after the 2011 quake in Japan. The shaking lasted six full minutes. The entire Olympic National Rain Forest disappeared beneath the ocean. That leaves the major cities such as Seattle, Tacoma and Olympia vulnerable to a massive tsunami wave that's expected shortly."

"Have mercy, Lord," Kenny whispered, her voice full of dread. Her mind still dealing with horrific scenes from the dream she'd experienced, while trying to comprehend the enormity of the situation that lay ahead.

Each day brought news of chaotic situations arising worldwide. Judging by the news stories coming out of the US, Kenny didn't think she would recognize the place any longer. Highly organized incidents were used by the elite to incite race wars and the murder of many police officers. Angry mobs roamed the streets. Rumors of martial law being instituted and the disarming of citizens filled the air ways on social media.

Tornados cut wide swaths of destruction across middle America. Flooding in the southeast destroyed thousands of homes. Sink holes opened up in various locations, swallowing homes businesses and roads. Terrorist attacks like the bombing at the Boston Marathon, San Bernardino and Orlando, Florida, where many lives were lost was becoming common place.

And that was just America; ISIS inspired terrorist attacks had hit France, multiple times. Belgium's airport was bombed killing many and on and on it went. ISIS continued to move across the middle east slaughtering, raping, beheading and burning alive the Christians in the area. How they thought these actions could guarantee them a place in heaven, Kenny just didn't understand.

Those pushing hard to birth the New World order, were experts at bringing about the chaos necessary to achieve their goals. Things were happening so fast now it was difficult to keep up. The beast was on the rise.

And now the literal geography of the US would change. Her uncle had warned that if the president of the United States actively worked to divide any part of the land of Israel, America would be divided as well. She'd thought her homeland already divided ideologically, however she'd never imagined the landscape would be forever changed as well.

"Oh God," Theo whispered as if in pain, "Please, Father, help the people of Washington state. They need you, Lord. Divert the tsunami away from the major cities, Father. Protect those who belong to you..."

Kenny heard her uncle praying as she moved with Lily toward the kitchen table to view the computer screen that all were watching intently.

"The San Andreas fault is rumbling," Ned broke in excitedly.

"What magnitude," Theo asked sounding distressed.

"The ticker at the USGS is climbing, six, seven," he paused as the ticker slowed. "It's showing the earthquake at 7.9."

"They're registering a 5.0 in Panama City," Kenny observed out loud.

"Brace yourselves," Theo warned ominously, "This area is part of the ring of fire, and the movement is coming in this direction."

Turner came to her then, “Elijah headed south yesterday, and we are nearing the tip of South America.”

“Will we round the tip before the tsunami reaches us,” she inquired soberly.

Shaking his head his glance wandered, “I don’t know. He’s giving it all he has but…we don’t know if it will be enough.”

His turquoise glance found hers once more. “If this is the end for us, I want to say two things; I thank God that He gave me a fleeting glimpse of what home and family were truly meant to be. I love you, Kenny. And, I’m sorry that telling you of our concerns caused you so much grief. I just thought if you knew how much danger you were in that you’d be more careful and not take off on your own.”

Kenny nodded, “I know you were just trying to protect me, and the baby.” After that dream or vision, whichever it was, she knew their concerns were not unfounded. In her heart, she knew the Lord was trying to show her what the evil one’s vile plans were.

Silently, Kenny decided that if they survived the tsunami, she would tell them of her dream. She could see no need to add stress to their already chaotic situation by telling them now. If they didn’t survive they would be with the Lord, and it wouldn’t matter, then anyway, she mused.

Emma rushed into the room from the helm. "Elijah told me to tell you he just reached the Strait of Magellan. He wants to know if there is any word on the tsunami."

"What are they saying," Theo inquired of Ned, who was pouring over the information on the USGS website.

"A thirty-foot wave just slammed the new coastline of Washington State. They're predicting several million will die. The San Andreas fault has also reconfigured the California coast. A powerful 8.2 quake just hit off of Iquique, Chile..." Ned reported excitedly and turned facing Emma. "Tell Elijah we're likely to face at least a twenty-foot wave in the next thirty minutes. He needs to step on it. If we can make it to Port Williams, we might survive."

Obviously dismayed at the news, Emma ran from the room back to the helm to relay the information.

"Is there anything we can do to prepare for this," Kenny questioned her uncle.

Theo drew in a deep breath and released it slowly. Reaching out he clasped her left hand, "We can pray that the Lord will have mercy on us. And, ask Him to give Elijah special wisdom for this circumstance."

Everyone's head bowed as Theo led them in prayer. "...Father, if it is our time, we'll see you in just a few minutes. However, if there is more you would have us do, calm the waters like you did on the Sea of Galilee. Give Elijah insight on what he must do to save this ship. Lord, we love you and we thank you for never leaving nor forsaking us, in Jesus's name, amen."

Giving her husband a thin-lipped smile, Kenny wrapped her arms around his neck. Feeling his arms encircle her, she whispered by his ear, "I love you, Turner. If we go to heaven this night, look for me. And then, we can find the children."

Pulling back slightly his loving glance poured over her face a couple of times, "It's a date," he confirmed with a smile. And then he pressed his lips to her forehead ever so gently.

"Ned," Theo said then, "can you get one of the drones' ready to go? It might help Elijah to know what to do, if he could get a bird's eye view of the tsunami."

"Sure," he answered and leapt from his chair. "I'll get Emma to help me," he informed as he dashed toward the helm.

"Is there something the rest of us can do," Lex inquired.

Theo looked round the cabin and nodded. "I think it would be good to gather all the pillows and blankets and bring them in here. These sofas are bolted down and away from the windows. We can hunker down between them and use those items to buffer us, so we won't get slammed around."

"Yeah, that sounds good," Turner affirmed, "and there's room for all of us."

Each member of the team scurried off to grab the things Theo requested. Soon they had them piled on the couches at the ready. Ned and Emma had one of the drones on the table and linked it to the laptop so they could control its movements.

"Is it ready to go," Kenny heard Theo inquire with urgency as he watched them working.

Ned's fingers moved rapidly over the keyboard as he intently studied the computer screen. "Yes," he responded as he picked it up and walked to the back of the ship. Pressing a button on his laptop he released the drone. It took off immediately.

The sky was just beginning to brighten with the early-morning light. Ned came back inside the cabin. "You need to gather in your safe place. I'm going up to the helm, so I can feed Elijah the info we get back. I've linked Cindy's laptop to the feed from mine. You'll be able to see exactly what we see, if you want to that is."

Pursing his lips, Theo nodded his appreciation as he accepted Cindy's laptop.

"Thank you," he said quietly before Ned turned and left the room.

"Let me help you," Kenny offered when she saw her uncle gripping his mid-section in pain. He was attempting to lower himself down to the floor between the sofas. That water cannon, or whatever it was, had obviously done some real damage.

"Kenny, let Lex and I get on either side of him and lower him down carefully," Turner suggested.

"Alright," she answered agreeably and stepped out of the way.

They laid him down with his face toward the floor at the center of the space between the couches. Lex and lily stretched out together to Theo's left. Turner put his back against the opposite couch, and Kenny laid down next to him and to her uncle's right.

They worked together and stuffed the blankets between each person to give them some cushioning. It wasn't much protection, Kenny thought silently. However, it would keep them from slamming directly into one another.

Theo was about to open the laptop when he reached under the sofa and pulled out a piece of paper.

"What is it," Turner quizzed.

"It's the missing note that your wife left for you," He said as he handed it to him. "Perhaps a breeze sent it flying. Anyway, it doesn't really matter. You trusted her word that she'd left you a message about where she was going, right?"

Kenny glanced over her shoulder at her husband wondering how he would respond.

He released a sigh of exasperation, "I know it didn't sound like it at the time, but I did believe you when you said you'd left a note. It's just that I was so concerned that some of those evil buggers had gotten their hands on you again," Turner explained apologetically. "I'm sorry, Kenny. I didn't mean to embarrass you or hurt you."

"I know," she whispered and smiled. "I should have waited a few minutes until your meeting was over to tell you of my plans. It's just that I got so accustomed to taking care of myself, and being on my own. I still sometimes have trouble remembering that is no longer true. I'm sorry I made you worry."

His turquoise glance washed lovingly over her face before he gently kissed her forehead. "If we are to die today, there's something more I want to say to you," Turner's voice was choked with emotion as a line of moisture became visible in his eyes. "You're the best thing that ever happened to me. You are my love, my family and my home. I would gladly fight to the death to save your life. But sweetheart, in order to do that I have to know where you are.

"If we survive this ordeal, promise me someone will always know where you're at. I believe Theo is right about one of those critters having a fascination with you for many years now. We're not trying to frighten you; we just want you to know why you need to be more careful, alright?"

With tears slipping from the corners of her eyes, Kenny nodded in agreement. "I understand, and believe me; I have no desire to be in their company ever again. What I can't comprehend is what they think they could do with me since I belong to Christ. After the ordeal with the reptilians, you told me about the power of the expressed word. Everything that was created was fashioned through the spoken word of God. The Bible tells us that we are to be imitators of God. And Jesus gave the example when Satan took him into the desert to test him. He replied to Satan's temptations by saying, it is written, and then gave a Bible verse appropriate for that circumstance."

Shaking her head thoughtfully, she said, "I can't tell you how many times I whispered, no weapon formed against us shall prosper, since we left Panama City."

When she looked at her uncle, he was smiling. "We will need to be firm in our faith and walk with the Lord until He calls us home," he said as he glanced at the newlyweds on his left. "The four of you are newly married. So, you have recently experienced that kind of all-consuming love that comes at the beginning of a relationship. Our love for Jesus should be like that. We should desire to be in His presence and want to talk to him at every opportunity. He gave his life for us when we were still living in sin and enemies of God. He loved us more than we know how to love. When he looked at us, he could see how lost we were. And he knew that unless he made the ultimate sacrifice, we would be eternally lost in our sins. So, he willingly laid down his life for us that we might be saved and forever be with the Lord.

"Things are likely to get very scary," he released a huff of a laugh then. "Yes, even more than they have been. We must focus on the love of Jesus. And the power we have in his name. We can do all things through Christ Jesus who strengthens us..."

14

"Theo," Ned's voice could be heard as his picture appeared in the upper left-hand corner of the computer screen. "We've spotted the tsunami wave. It's not as bad as I thought it might be. Probably since we're at the tail-end of the movement in the ring of fire. Still, Elijah is going to have to climb up a twelve-foot wall of water."

Theo nodded, "Okay, how soon do you think it will reach us?"

"If you look at the screen I'm sending you the feed from the drone. My guess would be in about five minutes. May God bless us all and keep us safe."

"Amen," they all responded simultaneously.

The room grew very quiet as they observed the wave approaching for several moments. Kenny gripped her husband's hand and pulled his arm over her. If it was their time, she wanted them to go together.

The drone footage showed Elijah approaching the wave at a forty-five-degree angle. They could hear the engine revving as they began the arduous climb. The water churned and roared like an angry monster.

"Help us, Jesus, we need you," Theo whispered fervently; his eyes glued to the computer screen.

The higher he climbed up the face of the wave the greater the angle of the boat, soon they would be literally vertical. Kenny closed her eyes, "I trust you, Lord," she whispered. "If it is our time, we'll see you in a few minutes, if not, you'll safely take us over the top of this wave. Either way, our lives belong to you, my Lord and my God."

"Brace one of your feet against the metal leg of the couch," Turner urged Lex. "I'll do the same on this side. Everyone, hold tight to the person in front of you."

Both Lily and Kenny wrapped their arms tightly around Theo. Looking over her uncle's shoulder, she could see they were approaching the top of the tsunami wave. Suddenly, the roar of the vessel's engine died and there was no sound at all. Kenny closed her eyes tight, and rested her head against Theo's shoulder. She was certain they would enter the presence of the Lord at any second. The silence seemed to last forever.

Turner's arms tightened around her, and she could hear the whispered prayers of the others. She anticipated a crash as the wave swallowed the ship. And then, the engine roared back to life. Gravity had been tugging at them the whole time causing them to slip toward the back of the boat just a little. All at once, Elijah's yacht leveled off; they were horizontal once more.

Kenny glanced quickly at the laptop. Her light-brown eyes wide with wonder, she was amazed that they appeared to be sailing on a calm sea.

"What happened," she beseeched her uncle who was shaking his head, seemingly astonished.

"It was like the hand of God picked us up out of harm's way and gently set us back down. We encountered the tsunami, just as we reached Cape Horn at the southernmost tip of South America. According to current GPS readings, we are now 529 miles from our former location."

Getting to her feet, thankful to be alive, she watched as Turner and Lex helped her uncle to his feet. Moving to the windows in the cabin area she looked out to find a very familiar and unsettling landscape. Her brows furrowed when she noted that the land they were approaching was covered with ice and snow. Some bare patches of ground were visible, and they were covered with rocks. Huge chunks of ice floated in the water; some were covered with penguins.

"What is this place," Kenny whispered, trepidation sounding in her voice.

"We are approaching the South Shetland Islands, near the Antarctic Peninsula," he explained.

"Antarctica," Kenny repeated quietly as the disturbing aspects of her dream came flooding back.

Turning toward her, Theo studied her face with his concerned gray eyes. "That's right," he assured sounding hesitant, "what's the matter?"

Observing her uncle's face, she looked for any hint that he knew the secrets of what lay beneath the ice of Antarctica. Surely in all their travels and the considerable research they'd done over the past ten years, they'd learned of the covert operations underneath this frozen tundra. She reasoned.

His gray eyebrows rose high up on his forehead as his eyes narrowed on her. "Sweetheart, tell me what's bothering you."

Her expression fell, "During this time since the RFID tag was removed, and everyone insisted I rest; I've been doing some research. I came across some very disturbing facts about Antarctica. We need to get out of here before they become aware of our presence. This is a vile and wicked place."

"Kenny," Turner said her name as if he were going to try and allay her fears.

"Turner, please..." she pleaded, holding up her hand as if to halt his progression. "I assumed that you and my uncle must have found this information during your many years of study. I just figured that despite the fact, this material wasn't in Theo's notes, you had to have come across it at some point. I mean if I could find it..." Kenny stopped in mid-sentence, feeling flustered because she didn't feel as if she were making much sense. She also felt overwhelmed by a sudden sense of urgency about departing from this place as soon as possible.

"Calm down, sweetheart," Theo encouraged, "and tell us what you know."

Feeling that every second they lingered put them in mortal danger, Kenny knew she had to make her point quickly.

"There are giants here," She blurted out. "I saw them in a vision the Lord gave me while I was in the bedroom. The one who wants to claim me for his own is here."

"What," Turner broke in fiercely, "Are you sure?"

Nodding, she couldn't stop the tears from slipping down her cheeks. "I'm sure, Turner. This is what he said; Come to me and I will take you to a place where you will be warm and worshiped. Join with me and I will give you powers above that of mere mortal men. I will share with you the forbidden knowledge of heaven."

A mixture of anger and fear came across his face. "What else did you see," he asked through clenched teeth.

"Below the ice, there exists a massive underground facility large enough to house a Titanosaur. Do you remember our conversation at Miguel's that last morning we were there? Remember the noises we heard, and how we thought it sounded like the dinosaurs from Jurassic Park? As far-fetched as it may seem they have brought them back. The giant rode this massive creature like one would a favorite horse.

"I saw high government officials and presidents. They all came to observe an eclipse of the sun. When it was full, a bright white light was visible at the upper left of the sun. The kings and rulers of the world began chattering excitedly about planet Nibiru. I couldn't understand everything they said, because I was a watching them from a distance, trying not to be seen.

"And then, strange flying ships swooped in. Most of them hovered overhead, but one landed on the ice. Men dressed in Nazi uniforms came boiling out of the ship like ants from an ant hill. The giant ordered them to find me and to bring me to him."

The members of the team glanced at one another, seemingly distressed by her words.

"Kenny, don't get angry with me." Her husband began somewhat reluctantly. "Isn't it possible that you were having a nightmare because we told you we thought one of those critters had designs on you?"

Elijah entered the cabin then saying, "My efforts to outrun the tsunami caused a bit of damage to the ship. It will take some time, but I do have the parts to fix it. However, I'll need the strength of some of the younger men on board to accomplish it."

"We have to leave now," she nearly shouted as a wave of goose bumps washed down over her arms. "You don't understand; I can feel them already. It's the same way I felt while the reptilians held me captive at the abandoned military base. Only it's much more powerful now than it was then."

Elijah's dark-brown eyes washed over her face; he seemed a bit taken back by her outburst. "Honey, as much as I'd like to be able to give you your wish, we are essentially dead in the water until that part is replaced."

Kenny's head bobbed forward, "Oh God, my God, please hide us from the evil one," she pleaded emotionally as she spread her hands protectively over her abdomen.

"I'll help you," Lex said then addressing Elijah, "we've got to hurry with the repairs. We're in danger here."

Turner came to her and gently pulled her into his arms. "I'm going to go and help them, so we can get the repairs done swiftly. Stay here with Theo and Lily." Cupping her face in his hands, he tenderly kissed her forehead. "Try to calm down, sweetheart, for your sake and the baby, okay?"

"I will," she assured, trying to smile but not quite able to pull it off. "I love you," she whispered meaningfully as he started to leave, feeling uncertain she'd ever get the opportunity to tell him again.

Halting his departure, his glance washed over her face, he seemed reluctant to leave her.

"Maybe, it was just a bad dream," she said then hoping to comfort him.

A slight smile appeared at the right corner of his mouth, "You don't believe that though, do you?"

Her glance dropped briefly. She wanted to say yes, but she couldn't lie to her husband. Giving a quick shake of her head, she looked him in the eye, "No."

Turning he left to help the others. She regretted that he was now fearful for her and the child.

"Sweetheart," Theo put his arm around her shoulder. "Why don't you come over to the table with us. If Lily wouldn't mind she could make some coffee, and we could talk while the others work."

"I started some right after we were once again horizontal in the water," Lily said then just as Ned and Emma came into the cabin. "It's almost finished."

"Is it alright if we join you," Emma inquired. "There is only so much space within the area where they're working, and we were just in the way."

"Of course," Theo began.

"Is the drone still with us," Kenny broke in.

"Actually, it is," Ned confirmed. "I was just about to ask Theo if he wanted me to bring it back to the ship."

"Do you want us to fly it over the Antarctic to see if we spot anything unusual?" Theo questioned.

"Yes, please," Kenny beseeched her uncle, "It would put my mind at ease."

"Alright," Theo agreed, "You heard the lady, let's do a once over."

"Okay," Ned said as he, and Emma sat down at the table, and opened his laptop.

His fingers moved quickly over the keyboard as he programed the drone. Emma sat next to him watching his progress.

"You realize this will take some time," Ned informed. "Antarctica is the fifth largest continent on the planet."

"No, I...didn't realize that," Kenny answered quietly; for some unbeknownst reason, that bit of information bothered her.

"Until they replace that part, we've got nothing but time," Theo remarked with a shrug of his shoulders. "So, it really doesn't matter how long it takes."

"I can set it at a higher altitude so we will cover a larger area at once," Ned offered.

"That's a good idea," Theo granted just as the coffee was ready.

Lily put several coffee mugs on the table along with the air pot. "Who wants some," she inquired. Everyone but Emma raised their hand, so Lily began filling four cups with the steaming hot amber liquid. When she'd finished, she set a fruit bowl full of apples on the table.

Absently sipping her coffee, Kenny watched the computer screen with particular interest. She was searching for anything familiar from the vision.

A half hour, an hour and then two went by without anything unusual showing up on the monitor. Kenny was almost to the point of believing that Turner was right. Perhaps it was just a nightmare she had because of what they'd shared with her.

Elijah came into the cabin area wiping his hands with a towel. His sleeves were rolled up past his elbows and there was a grease spot on the side of his nose.

"The repairs are going much quicker than I anticipated," he shook his head seemingly amazed. "Those two young men are working feverishly to finish as soon as possible. With any luck, we will probably be done in an hour. I just came up to grab some bottles of water."

"I'll get them for you," Emma volunteered as she went to the cabinet under the sink. Getting three bottles she handed them to her uncle.

"Thank you, my dear," Elijah acknowledged. "I'd best get back and help them complete the repair, so we can get out of here." Looking at her, he wanted to know, "Are you feeling any better?"

"Yes, and I'm sorry for the way I growled at you earlier," Kenny answered, truly repentant.

"It's in the past, don't worry about it," he assured with a smile as he left the room.

"I really didn't mean to yell at him," Kenny said to Emma. She felt the need to apologize to her as well for the way she spoke to the girl's uncle.

Emma smiled and shook her head as if to dismiss her concerns. She opened her mouth to say something...

"What the hell," Ned sounded alarmed as he shot up from his place at the table. Falling backward over his chair his feet tangled in the charging cord for his laptop sending it slamming to the floor.

"What happened," Theo demanded, obviously concerned by Ned's reaction.

Turner looked at Lex bearing a scowl, "Did you hear that?"

"Yeah," he answered with concern as he immediately made his way up the ladder that led from the engine compartment to the helm.

Swallowing hard, Turner was fast on his heels. Apprehension filled him when they entered the cabin area. It appeared very dark inside the room, although he knew it was mid-day. They heard hysterical voices out on deck. Rushing past his friend, he made his way quickly toward the others.

They were obviously distraught as they looked upward. The huge UFO they'd seen in Panama City hovered silently overhead. No wonder it seemed dark, he thought, it must be nearly a half mile wide. He was suddenly hyper aware that his wife was not among the others.

"Kenny," he said her name fearfully.

Sobbing uncontrollably, Lily shook her head sadly, and wrapped her arms around his neck and hugged him tight. Dread filled him at witnessing his sister's emotional display.

"He's taken her," Theo managed in a tear choked voice. "She was with us at the kitchen table. All at once, the room grew dark, and then she disappeared right in front of us."

Hot burning tears instantly filled Turner's turquoise eyes and quickly streaked down his cheeks. The craft vanished into the thin air. Pushing back from his sister's embrace he rushed to the railing and searched desperately in every direction. However, there was no sign of the ship anywhere. Tormented in his spirit, he dropped to his knees.

"Father in heaven, protect her and the child," he pleaded. The depths of his agony sounding in his voice as, he wept, "She belongs to you, Lord. Show me where she is. You know me, Father. There's nowhere I won't go, nothing I won't do to rescue her. I would gladly give my life for theirs. Just tell me what you would have me do."

To be continued.

Influences

Paul & Heidi Begley
www.paulbegleyprophecy.com

The Alberino Analysis - The Book of Enoch, The Book of Giants, on You tube.

Tom Horn - SkyWatchTV.com, SciFriday Hosted by Derek and Sharon Gilbert. SkyWatch TV presents; Inhuman.

The Hagmann & Hagmann Report

Steve Quayle.com, genesis6giants.com

L.A. Marzulli - www.lamarzulli.net, www.watcherstv.com

BPEarthWatch – You Tube channel

The Septuagint - is a translation of the Hebrew Bible and some related texts into Koine Greek. As the primary Greek translation of the Old Testament, it is also called the Greek Old Testament.

Russ Dizdar, Shatterthedarkness.net

Made in the USA
Middletown, DE
10 August 2018